Archie Smith, Boy Wonder

A tiny voice asked, "Is he the one?"

This book, then, is suspicious. The stories you find here may have been written, as so many Burdick stories have been written, as the guesswork of authors drawn to Mr. Burdick's striking images and captions. But I believe these are the actual stories written by Harris Burdick, given by Burdick to the various authors who are now pretending to have written them. I have no proof of this theory, but when I questioned the authors involved, their answers did nothing to change my mind. Sherman Alexie told me it was none of my business. Jules Feiffer told me it was none of my concern. Lois Lowry told me she'd never heard anything so ridiculous in all her life. Louis Sachar told me he'd heard something equally ridiculous but that it was a very long time ago. Kate DiCamillo told me to talk to her lawyer. M. T. Anderson told me to talk to his doctor. Tabitha King told me to talk to her husband. Stephen King told me to talk to his wife. Cory Doctorow told me I should ask Walter Dean Myers, who told me to go bother Linda Sue Park, who directed me to Gregory Maguire, who told me that he had a special message from Chris Van Allsburg, which was to go away and leave him alone and stop talking about Harris Burdick. Finally, Jon Scieszka told me that he would be happy to answer my questions, and to please come in and have some ice cream, and then after a long pause he fled through the window and left me alone and it turned out to be sherbet.

Perhaps it doesn't matter. Perhaps these stories were written by Harris Burdick and perhaps they were not. Either way, the mysteries of Harris Burdick continue, and if you open this book, you will likely be mystified yourself. As you reread the stories, stare at the images, and ponder the mysteries of Harris Burdick, you will find yourself in a mystery that joins so many authors and readers together in breathless wonder.

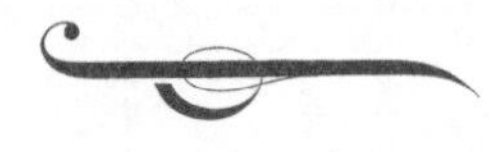

An Introduction by Lemony Snicket

Is there any author more mysterious than Harris Burdick?

Modesty prevents me from answering this rhetorical question, but the fact remains that Harris Burdick has cast a long and strange shadow across the reading world, not unlike a man, lit by the moon, hiding in the branches of a tree, staring through a window and holding a rare and sinister object, who cast a long and strange shadow across your bedroom wall just last night.

The story of Harris Burdick is a story everybody knows, though there is hardly anything to be known about him. More than twenty-five years ago, a man named Peter Wenders was visited by a stranger who introduced himself as Harris Burdick and who left behind fourteen fascinating drawings with equally if not more fascinating captions, promising to return the next day with more illustrations and the stories to match. Mr. Wenders never saw him again, and for years readers have pored breathlessly over Mr. Burdick's oeuvre, a phrase that here means "looked at the drawings, read the captions, and tried to think what the stories might be like." The result has been an enormous collection of stories, produced by readers all over the globe, imagining worlds of which Mr. Burdick gave us only a glimpse.

I always had a theory regarding Mr. Burdick's disappearance, however, that I have lacked the courage to share until today. It seemed to me that the mysterious author was hiding—but not in the places people usually hide, such as underneath the bed or behind the coats in the closet or in the middle of a field covered in a blanket that looks like grass. Mr. Burdick likely hid among his cohorts, a word that here means "other people in his line of work." Rather than give any more of his work to Mr. Wenders, Mr. Burdick might have distributed his stories, over a period of many years, among his comrades in literature. Perhaps he gave them as gifts in acknowledgment of their allowing him to hide in their homes. Perhaps he hid them in their guest rooms in the hopes that they would never be found. In any case, it was always my hope that the rest of Mr. Burdick's work would surface, even if the mysteries of Mr. Burdick—who by now is either very old, quite dead, or both—remained unsolved.

CONTENTS

For Peter Wenders, again

Houghton Mifflin Books for Children is an imprint of Houghton Mifflin Harcourt Publishing Company.

www.hmhbooks.com

The text of this book is set in Centaur MT.
Book design by Sheila Smallwood

Library of Congress Cataloging-in-Publication Data is on file.

ISBN 978-0-547-54810-4

Manufactured in Singapore
TWP 10 9 8 7 6 5 4 3 2 1
4500298309

The Chronicles of Harris Burdick

14
Amazing Authors
Tell the Tales

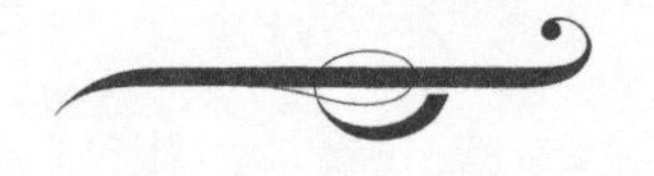

Chris Van Allsburg

With an Introduction by Lemony Snicket

Houghton Mifflin Books for Children
Houghton Mifflin Harcourt
Boston New York 2011

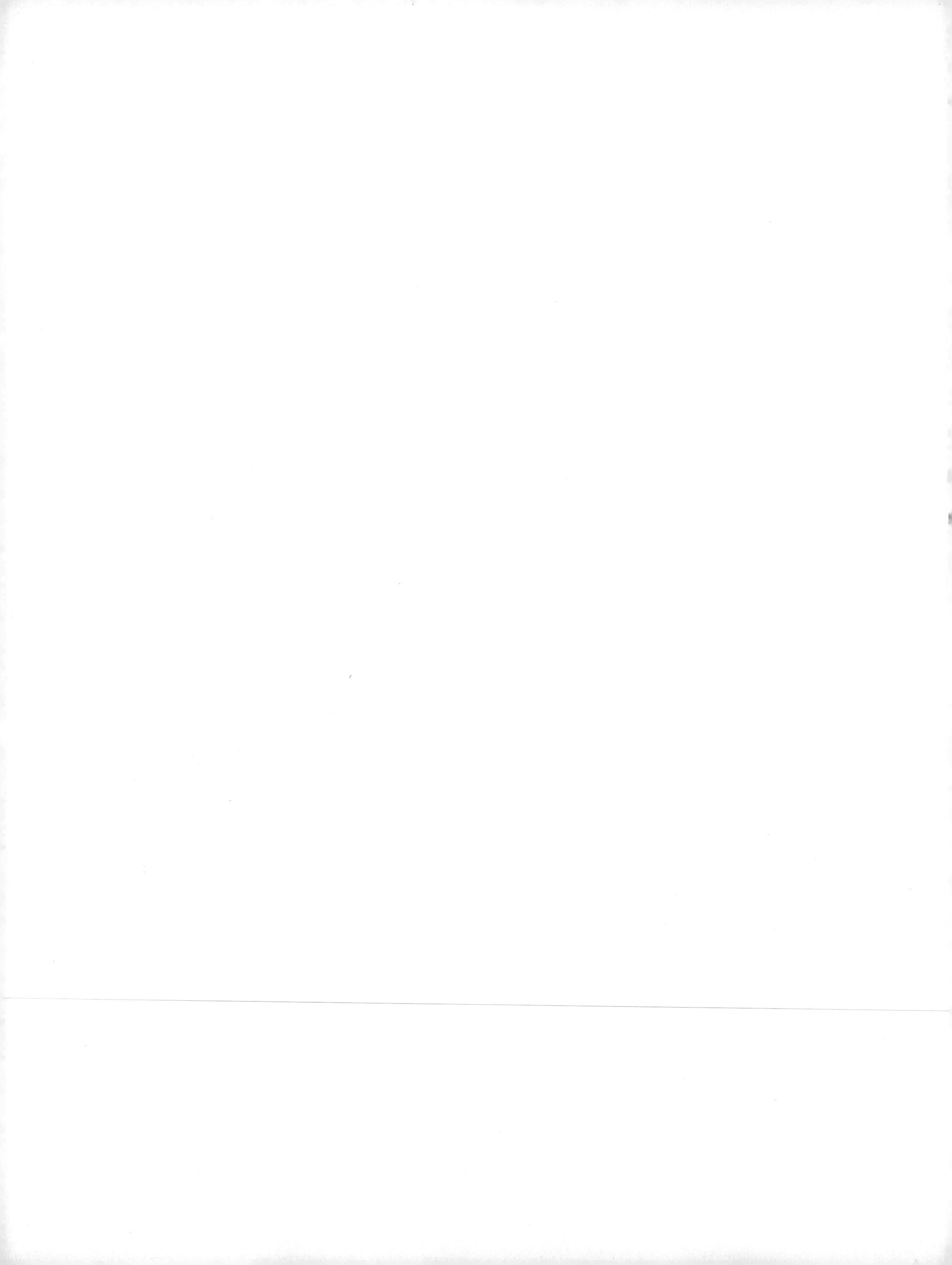

ARCHIE SMITH, BOY WONDER

TABITHA KING

Archie squinted into the glare of the sun as he choked the neck of the bat. He pulled his helmet down to get what little shade the visor gave. With his bad luck, the ball would be coming straight out of the sun, which seemed to sit on the runty little pitcher's shoulder. His palms were wet and gritty against the smooth ash of the slugger. His scalp, itchy and sweaty under the helmet.

The pitcher was shorter than he was. All the pitchers were. His bad luck again, he was the biggest kid in the league. It was a weird kind of leverage for them; if they sank the ball enough, it would come in at the low edge of his strike zone.

He thought about Luke in *Star Wars,* wielding his Jedi lightsaber against a tiny sphere of light. He took a deep breath and waited.

Behind him, the catcher tensed.

Not yet, thought Archie, his grip tightening, and then he thought, *Now* and his arm drew back just as a tiny sphere of light broke out of the sun. The ball met his bat with a glorious *CRACK!* and spun away back into the glare.

He stared after it even as the bat fell from his hand and he pushed off, the toes of his Converse All Stars digging into the dirt. There was no following it; that baby was gone. He reached first base, looking to make sure his foot touched it, but then he couldn't help looking up toward where the ball had disappeared as he ran all the way around the bases. He was running hard enough to make his chest tight, and he could hear people yelling to slow down—he could stroll if he wanted—but you don't do it that way, you always play all out, so he kept on running, tagging each base carefully and finally throwing himself down across home, so no one could ever dispute that he owned it.

Coach, who was kind of a goof, grabbed him and hugged him and pounded his back, screaming, "You put that one over the moon!" He screamed it three or four times as if nobody had heard him the first time.

Archie didn't need Coach to tell him what he had done. He was Archie Smith, Boy Wonder. Just like his mom said. There she was, jumping up and down and celebrating for him. He knew he was grinning too much and looked stupid, so he tried not to, but he couldn't help it. So what if people laughed at him because they thought he looked funny. So what, his mom always said. So what! When Archie wondered why she said it so often, in so many different ways, turning it into a joke, she said she got it from Metallica, this metal band his dad used to like.

Later that night, punching up his pillow, he replayed the homer in his head. He could just hear the baseball game in the park two blocks west. The moon was full; they hardly needed the lights. There was something really cool and magic about the idea: baseball by moonlight.

It was a grownups' game, guys from the bottling plant versus off-duty cops. Archie's mom had let him watch three innings and then he had had to come home and go to bed, on account of he had summer school tomorrow. His bad luck, special ed kids, him and a bunch of other dorks who had to go to school all year round because they were extra stupid. At least he could walk to school and didn't have to ride the short bus or wear a helmet all the time like a couple of the eds. His mom said that he wasn't stupid, that he was in special ed because he was dickslektic. He knew the correct spelling now but always thought of it the way he first heard it.

He had a desk calendar that had a big word to learn every day, and it was really cool, but he pretended he hated it, just to fool his mom because she was tough to fool.

He liked to watch the grownups play ball. They swore and yelled at each other and there was a yeasty smell of beer in the air. He wondered if the huge moon would ever sink into the pitcher's shoulder so that the ball would seem to come out of the moon. It was cool white, not hot yellow like the sun, so maybe the ball would move slow and smooth like cream when his mom was whipping it. Maybe it would be frosty cold to the touch, coming all the way from the moon through the night of outer space without the sun's heat pushing it like a fiery bat.

Impossible. Of course the moon was rising, so it was already higher than the pitcher's shoulder. The game would have to go on into tomorrow morning before the moon got low enough to sit on anybody's shoulder. It would probably sink to the top of some trees and sit there like a stuck balloon. The thought made him snicker. In his mind he moved the stars around into a baseball diamond.

Somewhere beyond the moon, a bat stopped a baseball with that beautiful *CRACK!* and Archie was back at the plate, feeling the force of the ball meeting the counterforce of the bat, the jolt starting in his wrist and moving along his arm back to where his shoulders were still swinging the bat. His whole body twisted as he threw himself against the driving force of the ball, his All Stars digging for leverage in the dirt and losing it; he was lifted right off the ground and hung there an instant while his heart stood still, like a big hand stopping the ball right there in midair. He hoped his mom didn't know about his heart stopping. The ball reversed itself, the bat busted thin air, and he came down on top of the catcher. He scrambled up, trying to see the ball, but it was gone or had burst into flame and become the sun. He closed his eyes against the coruscating light, but he could still see it through his shut-tight eyelids.

A tiny voice asked, "Is he the one?"

He pretended to be asleep; it was easy to do, just breathe long and slow so his mom would think he was conked right out like you had been hit by a foul ball.

"Who else?" a second tiny voice replied. "There's your Archie Smith, Boy Wonder, all right."

This voice had a different, well, range of colors to it, so he could tell it from the first voice.

The first tiny voice seemed to laugh; actually it sort of went incandescent, like a cap sparking off under a blow from a rock; pop and fizz.

"Why's he such a Wonder?" the second voice asked in its own crackly burst of color.

"His mom says so," said the first tiny voice.

They laughed together, so all the colors spilled and mingled like inks in a bowl.

He could see them through his lids, popping and fizzing and floating just over his head.

"It's because I always say 'I wonder' all the time," he wanted to tell them, but his throat and tongue were as numb as when the dentist gave him a shot in his gums.

"What does he mean: 'I always say "I wonder"'?" the second voice asked.

Archie thought: *They can read my mind.*

"Oh," said the first tiny voice, "he says, 'I wonder if I should wear my Boston Red Sox T-shirt today,' or 'I wonder if Miss Loomis will call on me to do my five-times,' or 'I wonder why regular kids have edges on their faces and big starey eyes,' or 'I wonder where baseballs go when they get slammed out of Fenway. I wonder if some lucky kid ever finds them.'"

Sometimes when Archie was pretending to be asleep for his mom and she looked too close when she bent over to kiss him, he would start laughing. His mom would laugh too, at his attempt to fool her. That was what happened now; his throat and tongue were all of a sudden okay. But he didn't open his eyes; the more he wanted to laugh, the tighter he squeezed his eyes closed.

"Bottom of the ninth," the second tiny voice fizzed, and he thought he heard a whole crowd of tiny voices popping and sparking and scintillating. Not very far away, either, maybe just outside his bedroom window, in the warm early summer night.

"Oh," said the first tiny voice, and he felt its fizzing and popping suddenly very close to his ear, almost inside it. "You should always wear your Red Sox T-shirt, if it's clean; Miss Loomis certainly will call on you to do your five-times, so you better work hard on them; regular kids don't have any choice about being regular, they just are, and every single one of them secretly thinks they look funny too; and once in a while, some lucky kid finds a ball that's been knocked out of Fenway, unless the moon's caught it and hurled it back, trying to tag the runner."

"Play ball!" cried the second tiny voice.

CRACK! And a ripple of *CRACK!*s like ice breaking up on the river in spring; cheers erupt from the park. Sparklers bursting into every crystal color in the universe.

Opening his eyes, Archie sat up and stared out the window, watching moonlets streak like shooting stars across the sky, headed for the moon, laughing on the billows of the summer trees. Slowly, one hand behind his head, he let himself down onto his pillow. Looking at the shadowy ceiling over his bed, he wondered. He wondered if his mom might let him go to the park tomorrow to look in the bushes for a baseball, maybe one the moon dropped, trying for the tag.

HB

Under the Rug

Two weeks passed and it happened again.

UNDER THE RUG

JON SCIESZKA

You should always listen to your grandma. It might save a life.

Grandmas say a lot of crazy things. Things like . . .

Look before you leap.
If the shoe fits, wear it.
Sit up straight.

So you never know what is really good advice and what is just crazy-talk. But grandmas know a lot. You should listen to them.

I should have listened to my grandma.

It started on Wednesday, five Wednesdays ago. I know it was Wednesday because Wednesday is sweeping day. Every Wednesday we sweep the house. Grandma and I. Grandma sweeps the kitchen. I sweep the living room.

At breakfast that morning, five Wednesdays ago, Grandma told me:

Hunger is the best sauce.
Let sleeping dogs lie.
That sweater and bow tie make you look like an old man.

I was sweeping and thinking that I like my sweater, I like my bow tie. Which is probably why I forgot the other thing Grandma always says:

Never sweep a problem under the rug.

I finished sweeping the living room. I put away the dustpan. I was just walking into the kitchen . . . when I saw the dust bunny under the couch.

I swept the dust bunny under the rug.

And I didn't give it another thought until the next Wednesday.

That morning Grandma said:

Never say never.
Don't count your chickens before they hatch.
What happened to that cake that was on the table?

In the living room, I swept up a trail of cake crumbs that disappeared under the rug. I lifted up the rug. The trail led straight to a clump of hair and crumbs and dust and two glowing red eyes that looked very angry.

The dust bunny had grown into a Dust Tiger!

I dropped the rug.

I couldn't tell Grandma, so I put the end table over the lump in the rug.

That worked sort of okay for about a week. Then the cat food started to disappear. Something got into the garbage under the sink.

I tiptoed into the living room. I peeked under the rug.

I saw a huge twisted knot of hair, dirt, liver-flavored Kibbles 'n Bits pieces, coffee grounds, orange peels, two chicken bone horns . . . and those angry red eyes staring hungrily at me.

The Dust Tiger had grown into a Dust Devil!

I dropped the rug in a panic.

The lump I had swept under the rug heaved. The lump growled.

I knew I had to take the bull by the horns. I had to strike while the iron was hot. I had to make hay while the sun was shining.

I dragged the bookcase over and dropped it on the bulge in the rug. Something squeaked. Something groaned. Then it was quiet.

The bookcase leaned against the wall a bit crooked, but everything was fine. Everything was fine.

I went back to sweeping every Wednesday.

Grandma went back to saying:

All that glitters is not gold.
Beware the calm before the storm.
Those pants make you look fat.

A week passed. Nothing happened. I might have dropped a few eggshells, a bag of stale cookies, and a turkey neck or two in a certain corner of the living room to keep things calm. There were no more outbursts, no more attacks.

Everything was fine.

Two weeks passed and it happened again.

That morning, Grandma said:

Silence is golden.
An empty barrel makes the most noise.
Where did that cat disappear to?

I followed a trail of cat hairs out of the kitchen.

I knew where this trail was leading, but I followed it anyway. I followed the trail into the living room. I followed the trail to the edge of the rug.

I slowly... carefully... lifted up one corner of the rug with the end of my broom. Nothing. A smudge of dirt, a single small tuft of red cat fur, a dusty copper penny.

Then it attacked.

A mad tangle of dust, dirt, fur, yellow hardened cake crumbs, moldy bones, eggshells, turkey necks, liver-flavored Kibbles 'n Bits, fingernail clippings, cat pieces, hair, fangs, and those two red eyes lunged for my leg.

The Dust Devil had turned into a Dust Demon!

I stopped the hungry monster's charge with the bristles of my broom. I flattened the awful thing with the smack of a chair. It heaved. It snarled. I swept it back under the rug.

I should have listened to Grandma. It could have saved a life.

But the Dust Demon needed more. And there was only one thing to do.

I remembered something else Grandma said:

Don't put off until tomorrow what you can do today.

I figured it was the least I could do, listen to her one last time.

I called, "Grandma? Could you come into the living room?"

HB

A Strange Day in July

He threw with all his might, but the

third stone came skipping back.

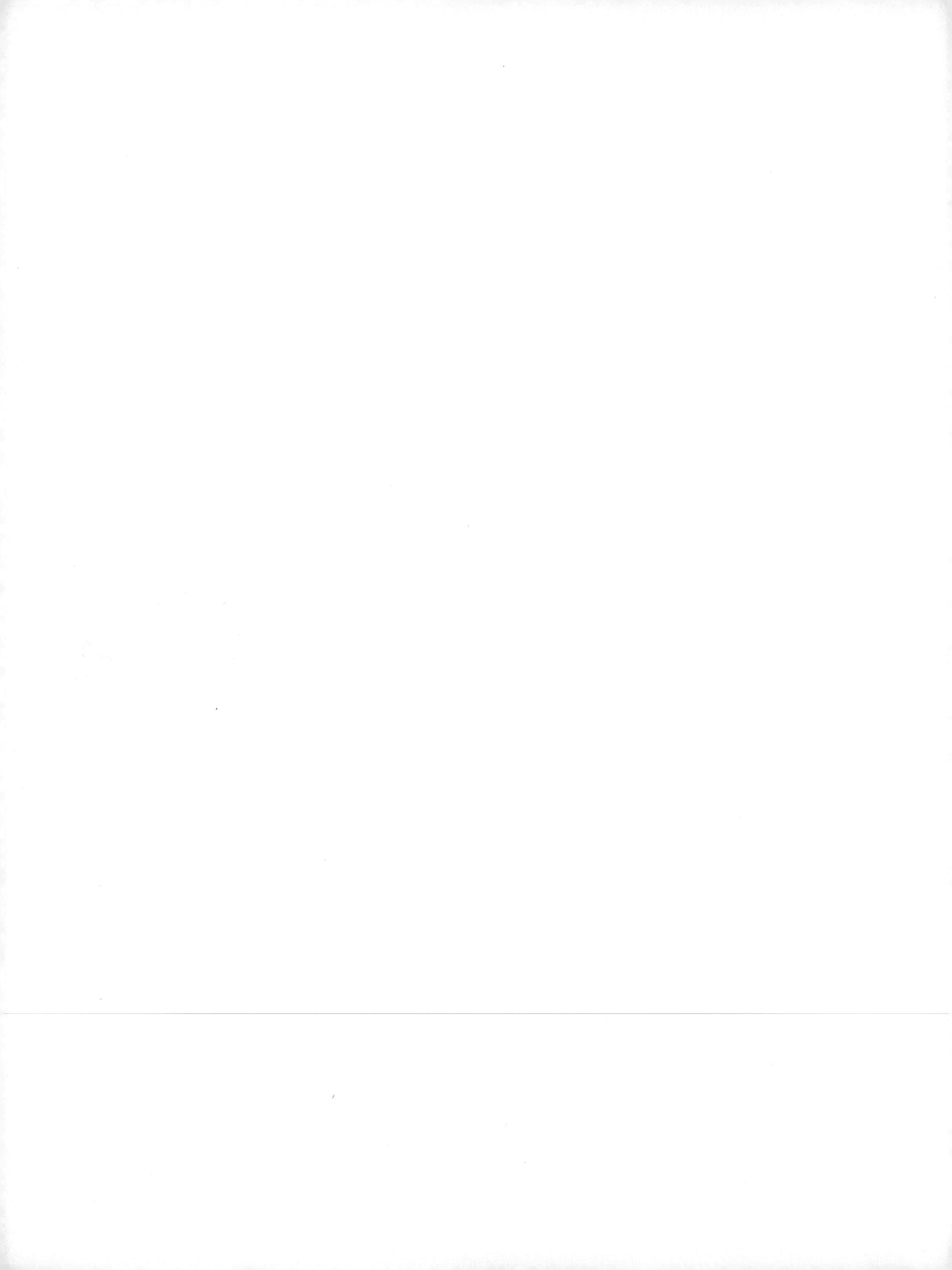

A STRANGE DAY IN JULY

SHERMAN ALEXIE

Because it was summer and it was hot and Timmy and Tina were ten years old, they sat on the park bench and slurped chocolate ice cream cones.

"When you get to the middle of your ice cream," Timmy said to Tina, "you're going to find a big white spider."

"When you get to the middle of your ice cream," Tina said to Timmy, "you're going to find a swarm of bees."

"Ha," Timmy said. "A swarm of bees couldn't fit inside an ice cream cone."

"They're the smallest bees in the world," Tina said. "And there's *three million* of them inside your ice cream."

"Well," Timmy said, "after you eat the spider in your ice cream, it's going to build a web in your stomach and catch all the food you eat, and you're going to starve to death."

"That's so gross," Tina said, and she just kept eating her ice cream. Timmy kept eating, too. They were brother and sister and they loved chocolate ice cream more than they loved each other. Heck, if they had discovered severed thumbs in the middle of their ice cream, Timmy and Tina would have just licked them clean and dropped them into a fish tank.

Okay, that's not true.

If Timmy and Tina had discovered severed thumbs in their ice cream, they would have screamed, thrown cones into the air, and run crying for home.

Or maybe not.

Timmy and Tina were very strange children. And maybe, just maybe, they might have been the kind of kids who enjoy finding severed thumbs in their ice cream. Yes, Timmy and Tina were exactly that strange. Everybody said so. Even their mother and father said so.

"My children," their father often said. "You are mine, and I love you, and you are so very cute and pretty, but you are aliens from a planet called Weirdatron."

When Timmy and Tina walked in the woods, the birds would shake their tail feathers and flutter their wings and sing, *strange kids, strange kids, strange kids.*

Okay, that's not true, either.

But Timmy and Tina scared birds. And they scared dogs. Heck, the lions at the zoo would cover their faces with their paws whenever Timmy and Tina came to visit.

Okay, that's not true at all.

But Timmy and Tina were the strangest kids in town. They might have been the strangest kids in the state. In the country. Maybe in the whole world. And they were strange in exactly the same way. And with chocolate smeared all over their faces, and all over his blue shirt and her blue dress, they looked exactly alike, too. Well, except for the fact that one of them was a boy and the other was a girl.

"Oh, look at you two," an old woman said to Timmy and Tina as she stopped near them. "I don't think I've ever seen a cuter set of twins in my whole life."

"We're not twins," Timmy said.

"We're triplets," Tina said.

"There's three of you," the old woman said. "How wonderful! Where's the other one?"

"She died," Timmy said.

"Oh, I'm so sorry," the old woman said. "Your little hearts must be broken."

"She was killed in a car wreck," Tina said.

"When we were five years old," Timmy said.

With tears in her eyes, the old woman pulled the kids close and hugged them. She wanted to squeeze the sadness out of their bodies. But she only managed to squeeze the ice cream cones out of their hands. And there's nothing more irritating than an ice cream cone dropped in the dirt. Well, except for two ice cream cones dropped in the dirt.

Timmy and Tina were very angry about the wasted ice cream. They were angrier than they'd ever been. You might think that Timmy and Tina would have been angrier when their sister died. But here's the thing: Timmy and Tina didn't have a sister, alive or dead. Timmy and Tina weren't triplets. They were only twins, which is still pretty cool, but not nearly as cool as being triplets.

"But why are you here in the park by yourself?" the old woman asked. "Where are your parents?"

"They died in the car wreck, too," Tina said.

"We're orphans," Timmy said.

They were lying, of course. Their mother and father, exhausted by their children's strangeness, were napping on a picnic blanket only twenty feet away.

"But who takes care of you?" the old woman asked.

Timmy and Tina looked at each other. They read each other's minds. They knew exactly what lie they wanted to tell. And they wanted to tell it together.

"We were adopted by an old woman," they said. "And we lived in a trailer house with one hundred cats. And the old woman fed the cats but she didn't feed us. And she whipped us, too. And sometimes she would pick up a cat, shake it until it was spitting mad, and then throw it on us."

"Oh, my Lord," the old woman said. "That's the most horrible thing I've ever heard."

"That's not even the worst part," Timmy and Tina said. "You know what's really horrible?"

"What? What?" the old woman asked.

"That old woman looked exactly like you!" Tina and Timmy screamed. They chanted: "She looked like you! Exactly like you! She looked like you! Exactly like you! She looked like you! Exactly like you!"

As they chanted, the old woman let them go and stumbled backwards.

"Exactly like you! Exactly like you! Exactly like you!"

The old woman turned and ran. Well, she was old, and so she really just walked as fast as she could. And her fast was slow, so Timmy and Tina were able to follow her easily.

"Exactly like you! Exactly like you! Exactly like you!"

So, yes, Timmy and Tina were strange. And they were cruel. They were strangely cruel. And they might have chased the old woman for a hundred miles. But it so happens that strangely cruel children get bored quickly. So Timmy and Tina let the old woman go. And they laughed.

"That was fun," Timmy said.

"It was sad, too," Tina said.

"Why was it sad?" he asked.

"Because I really wish we were triplets," she said.

"Yeah, that would be cool."

"You know what?"

"What?" he asked.

"We should pretend we're triplets," Tina said.

"Okay," Timmy said. "But how long should we do that?"

"We should pretend it," she said, "until everybody thinks we're crazy."

"No," he said, "we should pretend until everybody else goes crazy."

And so, later that night, after they got home, Timmy and Tina pulled an old dress out of her closet and took it with them to dinner. Timmy held on to the left sleeve and Tina held on to the right sleeve, and they skipped down the stairs with their imaginary sister, over to the dinner table, and gently draped her over a chair.

"Who is that supposed to be?" their father asked.

"That's our sister," Tina said.

"We're triplets," Timmy said.

Their father looked at the dress, at the imaginary sister, then at his wife. She shrugged her shoulders, as if to say, *This is just one more strange night in a lifetime of strange nights.*

"Well," their father said, "your sister looks rather skinny. She should eat something."

And so their mother filled five plates with chicken and potatoes and green peas, and four people ate well, but the fifth wouldn't eat a thing. She just stared at her food.

"Why isn't your sister eating?" their mother asked.

"Because she's mad," Tina said.

"Why is she mad?" their father asked.

"Because she doesn't want to go to school tomorrow," Timmy said.

Because they were weird kids and because weird kids were often punished, Timmy and Tina had to spend their summer going to school.

"Oh," their mother said. "I know that at least two of you have to go to school in the morning."

"If she doesn't go to school," Tina said, and pointed at the dress draped over the chair, "then I don't have to go to school."

"If you make us go to school and let her stay home," Timmy said as he also pointed at the dress, "then I will scream at the teacher until she cries."

Timmy was telling the truth. Three times in the last school year, he had screamed at his teacher until she cried. So what would be worse? A teacher weeping in the adult bathroom or two strange kids carrying around an empty dress at school?

"Okay," their father said. "Your sister has to go to school tomorrow."

"Don't tell us," Tina said.

"Tell her," Timmy said.

Their father sighed. He put his head in his hands. He wondered why he hadn't become an astronaut. He could be orbiting the earth, thousands of miles away from his strange life. But he loved his children. He did. And he loved his wife. He did. And he wanted to make all of them happy, so he did his best.

"Okay, young lady," he said, and pointed at the dress, "you are going to school tomorrow."

"Daddy," Tina said, "she's not going to listen unless you say her full name."

"Yeah," Timmy said. "Parents always use kids' full names when they're mad."

"Okay," their father said. "What's her name?"

Timmy and Tina laughed.

"She's your daughter," Tina said.

"We didn't name her," Timmy said. "You did."

"You and Mommy," Tina said.

Their parents looked at each other. What should they do? They read each other's minds.

"Okay, Mary Elizabeth St. Pierre," their father said to the empty dress. "You are going to school tomorrow. And I don't want to hear another word about it."

So, early the next morning, Timmy brushed his imaginary sister's imaginary teeth, and Tina combed her imaginary sister's imaginary hair, and they poured her a bowl of cereal she wouldn't eat and a glass of orange juice she wouldn't drink, and all three of them put on their shoes and raced to catch the bus.

On any other school bus in the world, it would have been strange to see a brother and sister carry an empty dress down the aisle. But this was Timmy and Tina's regular bus. They'd been riding this bus since kindergarten. So nobody was surprised by the strange behavior. In fact, most of the kids didn't even notice it.

But Timmy and Tina, being who they were, would not be ignored.

"Everybody, listen!" Timmy shouted. "This is our sister, Mary Elizabeth."

"Mary Elizabeth *St. Pierre,*" Tina added.

The kids all stared at the empty dress. Then they went back to their books and video games and cell phones.

"Okay," Timmy said. "If you don't all say hello to our sister, I am going to stand outside your bedroom windows and stare at you as you sleep."

Timmy had never done such a thing, but all of the kids figured he was fully capable of it, so they took him seriously.

"Hello!" all of the kids said to the empty dress.

"Say her name!" Tina shouted.

"Hello, Mary!" the kids shouted.

"Her full name!" Timmy shouted.

"Hello, Mary Elizabeth!" the kids shouted.

"Her fullest full name!" Tina and Timmy shouted together.

"Hello, Mary Elizabeth St. Pierre!" the kids shouted.

Timmy and Tina were very pleased. Mary Elizabeth St. Pierre was also pleased. She spun left and right and bowed. She was obviously a very proper and polite empty dress.

Soon enough, the bus pulled up next to the school, and Timmy and Tina and Mary Elizabeth hurried to their classroom. It's a well-known fact that empty dresses hate to be late for class. So Timmy and Tina rushed to their desks. They sat across the aisle from each other and held the dress like a flag between them. A blue flag covered with yellow flowers.

"Timmy and Tina," their teacher said, "what are you two up to now?"

"Three," Timmy said.

"Three?" their teacher asked.

"Three," Tina said.

"Three what?" their teacher asked.

"There's not two of us," Timmy said.

"There's three of us," Tina said.

"We're triplets," they said together.

Because of Timmy and Tina, their teacher had often cried in the classroom. She'd also cried during her drive to school. And she'd cried when she woke and realized that she had to drive to school. And she'd cried before she'd fallen asleep at night when she realized she'd have to wake and go to school again.

That's a lot of crying. That's a lot of tears. Ten million tears, to be exact. The teacher had counted them.

Their teacher's lips trembled. Her hands shook. Her heart was a radio blasting rock-and-roll at maximum volume. But she wasn't going to cry this time! No way! She would not let these strange kids make her weep in public ever again!

So she calmly walked up to the chalkboard and wrote the three hardest math problems she could think of. They were geometry questions, about squares and triangles and circles and three dimensions and a number that started out as 3.14 but kept going and going and going like an endless snake. These kids were only ten years old. She'd never taught them a thing about geometry. Not really. And certainly not about any math this complicated.

"Okay," the teacher said. "I would like three volunteers to come up and solve these problems."

All of the kids, even Tina and Timmy, froze. They knew they couldn't solve those problems. They couldn't figure out why their teacher expected them to know the answers.

"Timmy and Tina," their teacher said. "Would you, and your sister, please come up and work the board?"

Timmy and Tina groaned. They didn't want to do it. They were mad. But their sister was even angrier. Empty dresses hate geometry. Timmy and Tina looked at each other. They read each other's minds. They knew what to do. So they walked up to the chalkboard. Tina held a piece of chalk in her left hand and another piece in her right hand, which also held the empty dress's left sleeve. Timmy held a piece of chalk in his right hand and another piece in his left hand, which also held the empty dress's right sleeve.

Two kids and an empty dress! Triplets! With four pieces of chalk! And all four of them wrote the same thing in big block letters:

THIS IS NOT FAIR!

And it wasn't fair! Not at all! Timmy and Tina and Mary Elizabeth St. Pierre weren't bad kids, were they? No, they were rebels! They were fighting against an evil teacher!

"This is not fair!" Tina shouted.

"This is not fair!" Timmy shouted.

They shook the empty dress as if she were dancing. As if she were leading a parade.

"This is not fair! This is not fair! This is not fair!" Tina and Timmy chanted. And soon enough, the other kids joined with them. They all stood at their desks, pumped their fists in the air, and joined the protest.

"This is not fair! This is not fair! This is not fair!"

With the empty dress leading them, Timmy and Tina and the other kids marched out of the classroom. But because they were only ten years old, most of the kids stopped marching at the school doors, but Timmy and Tina kept marching. And chanting. And marching. And chanting.

They marched and chanted their way along the highway and out of town, down the dirt path, past a red barn, and to the shore of Lake Green. With Mary Elizabeth St. Pierre swinging between them, Timmy and Tina danced in the sand. It was a strange dance, of course. They jumped high in the air. They clapped their hands and clicked their heels. They made sand angels. They spun in circles and spat like sprinklers. They howled like wolves at the bright sun and the moon barely visible on the horizon.

"We are magic!" Timmy shouted.

"We are magicians!" Tina shouted.

"We can make anything come true!" they shouted together.

And then a strong and clever wind ripped Mary Elizabeth St. Pierre out of their hands and sent her drifting ten, twenty, thirty feet over and into the water, where she floated like a dress-shaped boat.

Timmy and Tina silently stared at the blue and yellow dress floating on the black water. It floated away from them.

"Don't you hate it when she does that?" Tina asked.

"Yeah, she thinks she's so much better than us," Timmy said.

"Hey," Tina shouted at the dress, "you're so stuck up! I hate you!"

"She's our sister," he said. "You shouldn't say that."

"But I do hate her," she said. "She always gets more attention than we do."

"Yeah, you're right," he said.

The dress kept floating away from them. It was going to float out of the lake and down a river and into and across the ocean and discover a new country. That dress was going to have adventures that Timmy and Tina would never be able to share.

Timmy and Tina were so jealous of their sister. They were furious with her.

"Throw a rock at her," Tina said.

"What?" Timmy asked.

"Hit her with a rock," she said. "And sink her."

So Timmy found a flat rock and skipped it once, twice, three times across the water and tore a hole in the dress.

"Good shot!" Tina shouted.

They watched the dress sink beneath the surface of the lake.

"Good," Timmy said. "She's gone."

But then the dress popped back up to the surface.

"No!" Timmy screamed.

"Throw another rock at her!" Tina screamed.

So Timmy found a bigger, flatter rock and skipped it once, twice, three, four, five times and tore a bigger hole in the dress.

"Yes!" Tina shouted.

"I got it that time!" Timmy shouted.

They watched the dress sink again beneath the surface of the lake.

"It's not coming back this time," Tina said.

"No way," Timmy said.

But, sure enough, that dress popped to the surface again. It almost seemed to float above the water.

"Timmy," Tina said, "I want you to kill that dress."

So Timmy found the best skipping rock anybody has ever found, and he skipped it twelve times and tore a fatal hole in the dress.

Or so he thought.

The dress didn't sink at all this time. In fact, it was now definitely floating above the surface of the lake. That dress was hovering above the water.

Timmy and Tina gasped in fear once, and then gasped again when the best skipping stone in the world came flying back to them, bounced off Timmy's chest, and landed on the beach at his feet.

"Did that dress just throw that rock back at us?" Tina asked.

"Back at me," Timmy said.

And then both kids screamed when that empty dress, when Mary Elizabeth St. Pierre, straightened her sleeves and hem and came floating back toward them.

"Stop her! Stop her!" Tina yelled. "She's going to get us!"

Timmy picked up the rock at his feet. He ignored Tina's panicked screams and took careful aim at their fast-approaching triplet. He knew they were in terrible danger if he missed. He threw with all his might, but the third stone came skipping back.

Missing in Venice

Even with her mighty engines in reverse,

the ocean liner was pulled further

and further into the canal.

MISSING IN VENICE

GREGORY MAGUIRE

He had lost himself. *The kid is lost.* That felt sour, to call himself "the kid." But that's what Scorpio Drake called him. "The kid is coming along? To *Venice?* Does he have to come, Candy sweet? Doesn't the kid have school?"

His stepmother had answered, "Scorpio. Of course he's coming. He's just lost his father. What do you think I'm going to do, park him in a kennel? Woof."

"Bark double bark to you, Candy darling."

Barf double barf to both of you, Linus had thought.

So once in Venice, he got lost. Every day. As lost as he could, while his widowed stepmother and her big fat old scorpion lawyer examined the jewelry in the safe-deposit box at the Banca d'Italia. Lost while Candace Mercurio and Scorpio Drake met with the Italian *avvocati.* Lost as lost, while they pored over legal documents with those nervous handsome lawyers like a nest of eels, writhing their sleek forms and wringing their narrow hands in their offices overlooking the Grand Canal. Lost on purpose the first two days; lost for real the third.

The kid. Lost in Venice. It served them right.

"He won't get lost," Scorpio Drake had insisted. "It's too early in the year for the school vacation crowds. Can't the kid read a map?"

Yes, the kid could read a map, even when most of the streets were water. But he couldn't read the laminated four-fold Venice-at-a-Glance map after he'd dropped it into the oily water under the thirty-fourth canal he crossed since his breakfast *ciocolatto* and *biscotti.*

Weirdly liberated—because who cared if he ever came back?—Linus wandered squares empty of all but thin, huddled trees. He ventured on bridges that changed direction two-thirds of the way across. He mounted staircases and descended others. Passed nuns and *carabinieri.* He asked neither for prayers nor for a police escort. He liked being lost in the city of floating *palazzi,* façades golden as champagne above black water.

Probably about noon—he was getting pretty hungry—he came upon a shadowy *fondamenta* where the water curiously smelled less of sewage and more of ginger and molasses. A crooked old woman stood at the back of her little roofed boat, shaking a metal canister. Flour on the water like snow. "Goodness," she said in respectable English when she saw him. "Ants in the supplies. I hope ants can swim." She wore a high French baker's hat. An old trademark for some European baking soda come to life. "Lost, I suspect. You need some lunch?"

He was about to say "Anything but pizza" when a silvery glint flew through the air. "Oh," cried the old woman, and "Oh," cried Linus. But they didn't see where the ring went.

"Did you hear a splash? Mercy! I hope no fish eats *that* ring! Imagine a nice *pesci puttanesca,* the flesh filleted on a platter and the ring found and fingered by some villain! It's quite valuable."

"How much did it cost?"

"I mean *valuable* in that I value it. It's a mighty unusual ring. Not your dime store, gimcrack ring. It's compelling. If it floats out to sea and a squid picks it up, they'll be saying, 'Beware of the squid that ate Sicily,' that sort of thing."

"Squids don't eat landmasses."

"Use your imagination. They might. But where *did* my ring go?"

"I didn't hear any splash," said Linus to Her Craziness, the Queen of Gingerbread.

"I've been looking for that ring for six months. It must have slid off my hand when I was grubbing for a fistful of flour to scatter at the bottom of a baking sheet. Maybe it flew onto the pavement?"

The walkway was cobbled with ten thousand stones. "I'll look in the chinks for you," said Linus.

"I'll bake you your own gingerbread house if you find it for me." She disappeared for a moment while he was on his hands and knees, hunting, and then she returned with a very American sandwich, peanut butter and Concord grape jelly. His favorite. How did she know?

It took several hours before he found the ring. Not so compelling as all that—just a plain silvery band. The local church bells were striking four o'clock. His stepmother would be starting to worry. Well, maybe she would.

"You've got it! Brilliant child. Give it here and I'll make you your gingerbread house."

"Use your imagination," he said, throwing her own words back at her. "What would I do with a gingerbread house? I'm just going to keep the ring."

Shrieking at him to stop, the dumpy old baker hurried down the gangplank, but it took Linus only a minute to lose her. He ducked through dusky alleys and darted over bridges that divided in the middle and settled themselves in halves on the other sides.

Candy Mercurio was pacing the salon of the Albergo Santa Chiara by the time Linus had found his way back. She was testy with him. "No court will release those jewels to a legal guardian who manages to *misplace* her *ward.* I was worried silly over you."

"I wasn't," said Scorpio. "What's that in your hand, kid?" The lawyer grabbed Linus's forearm and twisted it just enough to hurt, and the boy's hand fell open despite itself.

"Scorpio, really. Haven't you seen enough jewelry this week?" asked Linus's stepmother.

"Oh, Candy, you know me. Baubles are my little hobby. I love to string cheap rings on a thread and dangle them from window latches to catch the light. This one seems common enough, but I'll take it anyway."

"Hey, that's mine!" cried Linus. "I found it!"

"So did I. Right in your hand."

"Don't be greedy," his stepmother said to Linus. "It's the least Scorpio deserves. Helping us as he does. Kiss double kiss."

"Wink double wink," said the lawyer.

Stink double stink, thought Linus.

In their room, Linus hissed, "That's not fair, Candy. That was my find. Is he picking your pocket the way he just picked mine?"

"I've asked you repeatedly to call me Mother. Since your own mother died when you were born and your father's dead now too, there's no one left to object. Really. No boy calls his maternal unit Candy. It's unseemly."

"What's happening with the jewels that Nona Mercurio left Dad in her will? Is Scorpio stuffing them in his briefcase behind your back after you have them appraised? We'll need *something* to live on, Candy. Some kind of a home."

"You do your math," she said, "and I'll do mine."

"And he'll do his," muttered Linus. He claimed to be ill, which gave Candy a chance to whip out for a quick dinner with the creepy lawyer. Linus ate potato chips and drank *limonata* in their room.

He was lying awake in the dark when his stepmother came in. "We're almost done with the accounting. Tomorrow Scorpio will file our papers with the authorities and then we can go home. Stop faking sleep, will you? I know you're awake. I can't imagine you really think Scorpio would skim jewels out of our haul."

Use your imagination, thought Linus coldly. But all he said, just loudly enough to be heard, was "Snore double snore."

When he woke next morning, his stepmother was gone. She'd left a note. "Celebration lunch at noon today at a modest place in Arsenale di Venezia. That's the shipbuilders district. Find it on your map, and meet us at the Ristorante Europa on the Ponte Penini. We'll wind up this ordeal."

Great, thought Linus. *And I've lost my map.* But of course it wasn't the only map ever printed of Venice. He would locate another.

The concierge told him that to find another map, Linus would want the nearest newsagent. Easy. Left out the door, second *calle* on the right, cross the first bridge, turn left, turn right, second bridge on the right, through the archway of the monastery, take the middle *calle* of the three that leave the plaza on your left, then cross the third bridge, and halfway down, on the left: *Eccolò.* Impossible to miss it.

He thought he had gotten at least half of the directions right, but perhaps he'd turned left instead of right, or taken the second rather than the first bridge. The neighborhood got seedy, and one of those clammy Adriatic mists started to wisp in along the canals. When he smelled gingerbread, he began to worry. Then there she was again, her hand out and her face fierce.

"It is not yours," said the old woman. "It wasn't made for a child's hand. Give it back."

"I don't have it anymore," said Linus. "I'm sorry. It's gone missing."

"*You'll* go missing if you don't give it back to me."

"I was wrong to take it from you, but now it's been taken from me."

She said, "Come aboard my boat and we'll go look for it."

"I'm not supposed to talk to strangers."

"You're not supposed to steal, either. Come on." She grabbed his elbow and propelled him onto the gangplank. She was strong for an old woman. Though her vessel was only the length of the standard gondola, it sported a tiny cabin large enough for one, if he crouched down. Well, more like a bin—or a kennel—than a cabin. "Be my guest," she said, and kicked him in.

The smell of cinnamon and clove was overpowering. He nearly passed out. As he steadied himself, he realized that the room was much larger on the inside than it appeared on the outside. Space for a table and two chairs, an oven that steamed with baking gingerbread, shelves of supplies. Cabinets built into the walls. Bookcases, maps, navigational charts. A few gilded carnival masks, a lute, a dried squid nailed up by its tentacles.

A funny red cap was perched upon a plaster skull labeled "Phrenology of Talents." Pink highlighter letters marked out the cranium with sections of the brain: *Linear logic. Arithmetic skill. Muscle memory. Gender. Liver ailments. Guilt. Liberal tendencies. Affection. Double joints. Perfect pitch. Location of car keys. Balance. Verb tenses. Charms. Charmlessness.* And so on.

"That cap is worn by the ruler of Venice. It's a doge's cap—a *camauro.* You have a good head on your shoulders," she said, coming in behind him and examining his scalp with her knuckles. "Tell me how you lost my ring."

"I didn't precisely lose it. My stepmother's lawyer took it without my permission." She kneaded the truth out of him. All the truth. About his father's death. About his stepmother's worry about funds. About Linus's suspicion that Scorpio Drake would steal from them anything that Nona Mercurio, his father's mother, might have left them in her Italian bank.

The elderly woman swung open a shutter. She must have cast off; the boat was bobbing along the Grand Canal at *vaporetto* speeds. "We'll find him. I will have my way," she muttered. "I always do. Where shall we look?"

Linus told her about the meeting point in Arsenale di Venezia. "Good. We're nearly there," she replied.

"But I didn't tell you where I was going."

She laughed. "As if you know where you are going!"

Sure enough, just as they pulled up to a set of wet steps rising out of the canal, where they could tie up and disembark, along the *fondamenta* came his stepmother. "I told you never to go off with strangers!" said Candy at the sight of the old woman heaving herself up the steps.

How am I supposed to know the difference between strangers and family anymore? He didn't say this out loud. Turning to the crabbity old dame, he pointed to his stepmother and said, "This is Candy Mercurio."

"Candy *Lately*," corrected his stepmother. "I decided to go back to my maiden name, now your father's dead."

"Oh. Candy. This is . . ." He paused, unable to say "the Queen of Gingerbread." It didn't matter; she was approaching his stepmother.

"What's the matter, gingersnap?" the mysterious old dame said. Linus hadn't noticed that Candy's makeup was messy with damp.

"I . . . I thought I'd surprise Scorpio and meet him at the law offices. But he'd been and gone already, and taken the jewels, signing for them as my proxy."

"He'll be here soon," said Linus, without conviction. "He just got lost. Could happen to anyone."

"Oh, but the *avvocati* told me that after he left, they found a receipt for a single cruise ticket with stops in Rhodes, Marseilles, Naples, Mykonos . . . It must have dropped out of his coat pocket. I've been looking for him all morning—the hotel, the Caffè Florian at the Piazza San Marco. Then I hurried here, hoping he'd arrived early and was waiting for me—but he's missing, Linus! He's missing with our jewels! And that ship has probably left port by now."

I thought the jewels were mine, thought Linus. *But I should talk; I stole a ring, too.*

He glanced at the old woman. She looked at him as if she knew what he was thinking. Then with a curious expression she shrugged and reached out to hug his stepmother. "Poor lamb, you look as if you have a serious headache," she said, and Linus saw the old woman take the crown of Candy's head in her palm and press it down into her own shoulder. It was a consoling gesture, a sweet-old-grandma behavior, but Linus could see that the old woman was running her hand across the back of Candy's scalp, feeling the landscape of her character.

The old woman released Candy and said, "I know what you need. A spot of gingerbread to take your mind off your troubles. I have just the thing in my apron pocket." She pulled out a bit of gingerbread that looked as if it had been stamped out by a cookie cutter shaped like a scorpion. "Nothing like gingerbread to clear the mind, I always say."

Candy took it and began to nibble. Almost at once her worry and distractedness became more abstract, as if she were not really standing next to a Venetian canal eating a gingerbread scorpion but merely dreaming she was.

"Now," said the old woman to Linus, "whether or not that fiend is missing with your jewels, he's missing with my ring. I'm getting him back. Are you going to help or not?"

She might be a gingerbread fruitcake, but he owed her this. He listened as she babbled more nonsense. "This little exercise of the imagination works best for me when I'm peering through that very capable ring, but in the absence of *that,* we'll have to find a double for it." She eyed the canal. "Do you see the circle made by the bridge over the water?"

"The near bridge?" He squinted. She meant the circle made by the closest bridge and its reflection in the canal. *Bridge double bridge.* "Yes... It's more of an oval. It looks more like an eye."

"Like the eye of a squid big enough to eat Sicily?"

He wasn't going to answer that. Though in fact it did look like an enormous eye, seen from a fatal closeness.

"Ah, well. Think of it as the eye of a needle, then. Stand back, Candy Lately, or you'll be the late Candy Lately." Moving swiftly for an old biddy, she hustled into her cabin and then came out again carrying something warm from the oven and a bottle of something goopy. Molasses, by the smell of it through the wide mouth of the open jar.

"Are you watching?" she asked. Linus nodded. Candy was finishing off one gingerbread scorpion leg after another, lost in a bliss of imagined revenge.

"Ginger, molasses, clove, and salt," she murmured as she poured the molasses into the canal. "Lost my ring, but it's all his fault. Cinnamon, butter, flour, molasses. What a collection of pains-in-the—"

"Look!" interrupted Linus, who was leaning over the canal's edge to watch. Up from the depths of the black water something was floating. Something hinged and squarish. It straightened itself out, flat as an old-fashioned record album cover. The Venice-at-a-Glance map, emerging from the depths to serve as a floating platform.

"In case he doesn't remember how to get back to you," the old woman said to Candy, a little coyly. "Can't claim to be lost if a map's still floating around somewhere." She tipped the large jar of molasses nearly upside down. A single, final drop fell out into the water. "A little something sugary to lure a scorpion." It looked like a drop of blood in the canal.

Then she spoke a few words in Italian and the map drifted over to them. Kneeling, she set upon it a gingerbread pastry she'd brought from the cabin. It wasn't a gingerbread house or a gingerbread man, but the shape of a single human hand with its forefinger slightly crooked up, beckoning. *Come. Come.* A gingerbread hand.

"The rest is your job, because it's your fault he has my ring," said the Queen of Gingerbread to Linus. "Use your imagination, if you've got one. Pull into view whatever it is you most want to see."

He'd read *The Monkey's Paw*; he wouldn't wish to see his father again. He already held his father and his mother in his heart. Anyway, it wasn't a monkey's paw but a gingerbread paw! Ha double ha. Nervous stupid joke. When, really? Right now? What he wanted most right now was for something to work out, even though he couldn't think what that might be. Anything. Anything, after all the sorrowing.

"It's a bit of a way from the Bacino Stazione Marittima, the departure point for seagoing vessels. It's on the other end of Venice," admitted the old woman. "This'll take some doing. Keep concentrating." As if she didn't have a care in the world, she ambled over to Candy Lately and asked her what she'd thought of Venice—the Lido, the Titians and Tintorettos, the Murano glass, the gondoliers singing songs from *Phantom of the Opera*? Had she enjoyed her holiday? Candy answered with a singsong enthusiasm as if she'd contracted gingerbread amnesia.

Linus peered through the eye of the double-span formed by the bridge and its reflection. He tried not to become distracted by the sound of commotion, of demolition and screaming. A tidal wave in Venice? The ghost of Hurricane Katrina vacationing abroad? But concentrate she had said, so concentrate he did. *Pull into view whatever it is you want to see.*

Candy seemed not to hear the thundery menace. Her voice bounced thinly, like that of a stoned parakeet. "He took advantage of my misery! My lostness. I was looking forward to jewels to cheer me up. *Candy Lately,* back in business. Society columns. Hollywood blogs! Twitter-fests! 'Candy's back, and she's sweeter than ever!' Drake stole all that from me!"

Don't think about her. Just watch.

Around the corner of the canal beyond the bridge, a cruise liner like a great black iron football, ten stories tall, appeared. A coal-dark steel tsunami, crushing buildings to the left and right. Screaming, screaming, though the neighborhood seemed oddly empty of locals. No, the screaming wasn't human—it was the sound of motors at full throttle. To no avail. Even with her mighty engines in reverse, the ocean liner was pulled further and further into the canal. Linus saw to that. He saw to it through the flattened ring of the bridge and its reflection. He saw to it without blinking. He didn't blink, and neither did the bridge.

"Excuse me a moment, dear," said the old woman to Candy. She handed the large brown molasses jar to Linus. "You're doing fine, you. Native talent. You must have a big giant lobe for *aspiration.* Use this to scoop it up. Think of it as a glass kennel."

He guessed what she meant. He knelt down and floated the empty bottle in the water behind the gingerbread hand. He watched the boat shrinking in the darkly mirrored water. By the time it reached the near bridge, it was small enough to pass underneath without scraping. The buildings behind were straightening out, like wobbled reflections returning to order after a passing speedboat had jigsawed them up. The ocean liner now looked about the size of a gondola. A ship perfectly sized for scorpions on holiday.

It floated up past the gingerbread hand. One of the smokestacks was capped with a silver circle.

"There you go," said Linus. "Steady on now. There you are. That's my girl."

Shrinking faster, the ocean liner drifted neatly into the wide mouth of the molasses jar, all except the silvery tip of the highest smokestack, which snapped off. Linus caught it in the air and handed it to the old woman. When he went to retrieve the jar, he saw that the laminated map of Venice had sunk out of sight. The gingerbread hand was missing.

"You have very good eyesight," said the old woman approvingly. "Some call it second sight. Others call it double vision. I call it rare."

"What shall I do with the ship in the molasses bottle? Okay if I see if Candy wants it?"

"Ask her, if she's not too busy biting the hand that feeds her."

Linus turned. Improbably draped in the recovered jewels, Candy stood, blankly appreciative as if expecting no less, munching on a gingerbread thumb. The drama of the ambush of a villain and the miniaturization of an ocean liner seemed to have gone entirely unnoticed. Neither meanly nor sadly, Linus thought: *She never did pay much attention to me, either. Wish I could have meant something to her, but that's not my fault.*

He held out the bottle. "A souvenir of Venice?"

"I got the jewels," she said. "They'll have to see me through my other losses. Boo double hoo."

"I see," said Linus, and he did.

"I've got my ring," said the old woman, "but I'll take the ship too. You never know when an ocean liner will come in handy. We could feed it to a giant squid if we ever met up with one." The mouselike shrieking of a single voice was threading from the bottle, but the old woman fished a tin lid from an apron pocket and screwed it over the aperture.

"What about everyone else on that ocean liner?" whispered Linus.

"Munching gingerbread at the *stazione,* waiting for their vessel," she told him. "Don't worry about them. Ships are lost at sea all the time. So are boys. Shall I take you on board as an apprentice baker?"

"I . . . I . . ." He turned to Candy. But she seemed to have everything she needed.

"You owe me," the woman told Linus. "You stole my ring. I should demand seven years' indentured service. But I'll cut you a bargain. Three and a half."

"I don't know," said Candy, possibly not to him but to the Italian emeralds and rubies pooling in her hands. "You're very valuable to me."

"Think of it as sending him to school abroad," said the old woman. "Think of the sights he'll see!"

"Or you could just say I went missing in Venice," added Linus.

Candy seemed to have made up her mind. She was busy stuffing the jewels in her pockets. "Maybe Royal Ascot this year," she was saying. "The Cannes film festival. Opening the races with the Whitneys and Vanderbilts at Saratoga! And Mardi Gras in Buenos Aires. It'll be much better for you, kid, to have a stable school environment." She went teetering off. At the top of the bridge, Linus could see her reflection below. She didn't look monstrous in her reflection. She looked happy. Sad and happy.

"Well," said the old woman. She was squinting through her ring. "It doesn't seem to be damaged. You can't imagine what I was going to do to you if it got damaged. You haven't got *that* big an imagination."

"No, I don't," he admitted.

"But we'll make it bigger," she promised. "Travel is so broadening. Let's go. There's a girl on the Dalmatian coast that needs some coaxing off a cliff edge."

The mist had risen. She sat in the stern of the gingerbread gondola and smiled, neither fiercely nor warmly. In the reflection, she looked for a moment like Nona Mercurio. Daylight glinted on the water like diamonds at her neck, brilliants on her crown. But that moment passed double quick. They floated beside the slanting posts, striped like candy canes or barbershop poles. Past the great stone sugarloafs of museums, the basilicas like baked honey filigree.

Out into the lagoon, out toward the open sea, where, Linus practiced imagining, a giant squid was smiling to itself underwater, trying to open the lid of a molasses jar with its tentacles.

HB

Another Place, Another Time

If there was an answer, he'd find it there.

HB

Another Place, Another Time

If there was an answer, he'd find it there.

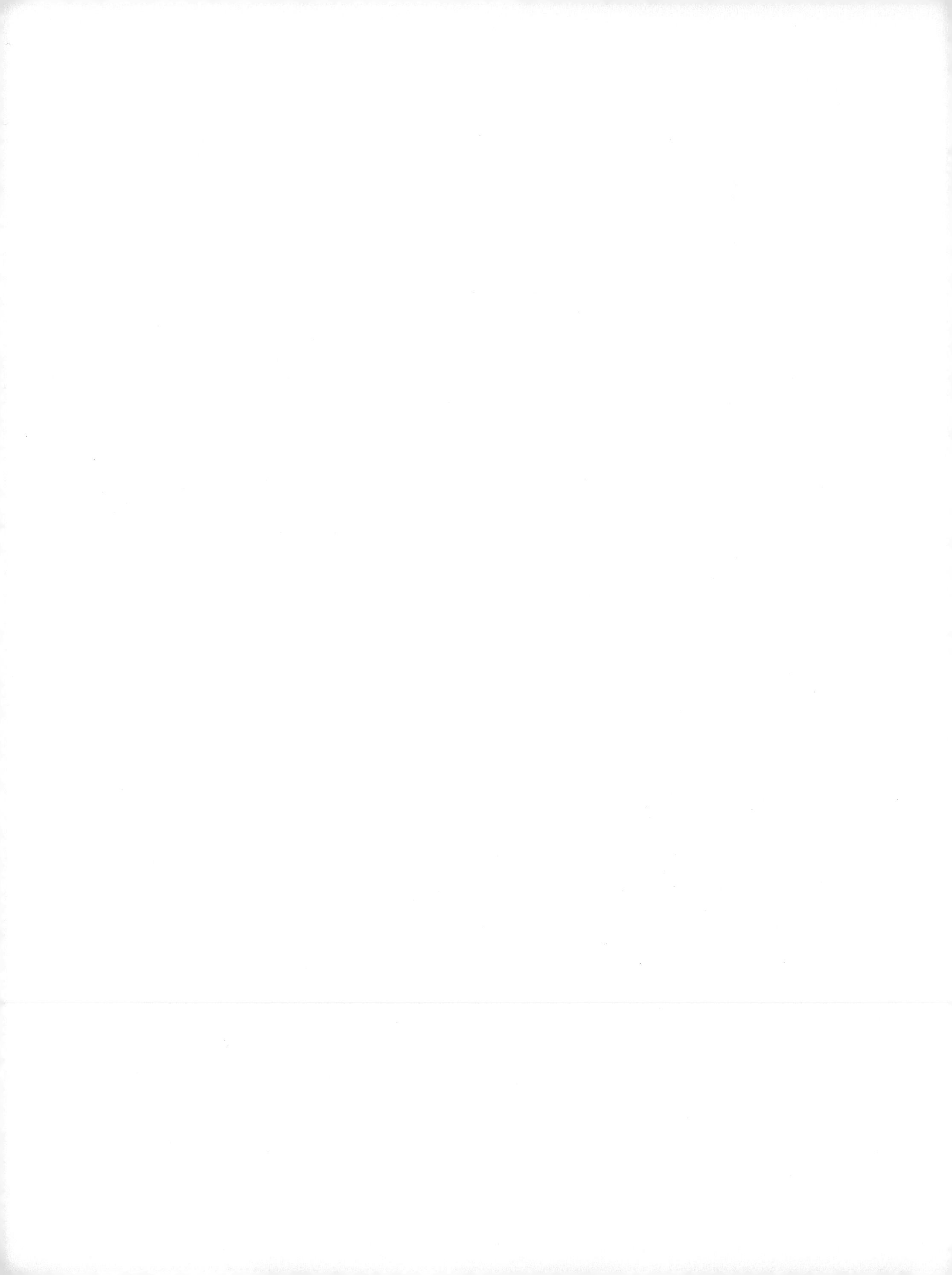

ANOTHER PLACE, ANOTHER TIME

CORY DOCTOROW

Gilbert hated time. What a tyrant it was! The hours that crawled by when his father was at sea, the seconds that whipped past when he was playing a brilliant game in the garden with the Limburgher children. The eternity it took for summer to arrive at the beach at the bottom of the cliffs, the flashing instant before the winter stole over them again and Father took to the sea once more.

"You can't hate *time,*" Emmy said. The oldest of the three Limburghers and the only girl, she was used to talking younger boys out of their foolishness. "It's just *time.*"

Gilbert stopped pacing the tree house floor and pointed a finger at her. "That's where you're wrong!" He thumped the book he'd taken out of his father's bookcase, a book fetched home from London, heavy and well made and swollen with the damp air of the sea-crossing home to America. He hadn't read the book, but his tutor, sour Señor Uriarte, had explained it to him the day before while he was penned up inside, watching summer whiz past the study's windows. "Time isn't just time! Time is also space! It's also a dimension." Gilbert thumped the book again for emphasis, then opened it to the page he'd marked with a wide blade of sawgrass.

"See this? This is a point. That's one dimension. It doesn't have length or depth. It's just a dot. When you add another dimension, you get *lines*." He pointed at the next diagram with a chewed and dirty fingernail. "You can go back and you can go forward, you can move around on the surface, as though the world were a page. But you can't go up and down, not until you add another dimension." He pointed to the diagram of the cube, stabbing at it so hard, his finger dented the page. "That's three dimensions, up and down, side to side, and in and out."

Emmy rolled her eyes with the eloquence of a thirteen-year-old girl whose tutor had already explained all this to her. Gilbert smiled. Em would always be a year older than he was, but that didn't mean he would always be dumber than she was.

"And Mr. Einstein, who is the smartest man in the whole history of the world, he has proved—absolutely *proved*—that time is just *another dimension,* just like space. Time is what happens when you can go up and down, side to side, in and out, and *before and after*."

Em opened her mouth and closed it. Her twin brothers, Erwin and Neils, snickered at the sight of their sister struck dumb. She glared at them, then at Gilbert. "That's stupid," she said.

"You're calling *Einstein* stupid?"

"Of course not. But you must not understand him properly. Space is space. Time is time. Everyone knows that."

Gilbert pretended he hadn't heard her. "But here's the part no one knows: why can we move through space in any direction—"

"You can't go up!" Em said, quickly.

"You got up into my tree house," he said, putting a small emphasis on *my*. "And you could go back *down,* too."

Emmy, who was a better fighter than any of them, put her fists on her hips and mimed *Make me.* He pretended he didn't see it.

"Why can we move through space in *almost* any direction, but time only goes in one direction, at one speed? Why can't we go faster? Slower? Backwards?"

"Sideways?" Neils said. He didn't speak often, but when he did, what he said was usually surprising.

"What's sideways in time?" his twin asked.

Neils shrugged. "Sideways is sideways."

"This is dumb," Emmy declared, but Gilbert could see that she was getting into the spirit of the thing—starting to understand how it had made him all so angry.

Outside Gilbert's house the summer roared past like a three-masted schooner before a gale, with all sails bellied out. Inside the study, the hours crawled by. And then, in between, there were the breakfasts and dinners with Gilbert's father, who was home for the summer, whose kind eyes were set into an ever-growing net of wrinkles and bags, who returned from his winter voyages each year a little thinner, a little more frail.

"And what did you learn today, my boy?" he said, as he tucked in to the mountain of lentils and beans made by the housekeeper, Mrs. Curie (who was so old that she had actually once served as Father's nanny and changed his diapers, which always made Gilbert giggle when he thought of it). Father was a strict vegetarian and swore by his diet's life-enhancing properties, though that didn't seem to stop him from growing older and older and older.

Gilbert stopped fussing with his lentils, which he didn't like very much. "Geography," he said, looking at his plate. "We're doing the lowlands." He looked out at the sunset, the sun racing for the other side of the planet, dragging them all back toward the winter. "Belgium. Belgium, Belgium, Belgium."

His father laughed and smacked his hands on his thighs. "Belgium! Poor lad. I've been marooned there once or twice. Land of bankers and cheesemakers. Like hitting your head, Belgium, because it feels so good when you stop. What else?"

"I *want* to do more physics, but Señor says I don't have the math for it."

His father nodded judiciously. "He would know. Why physics?"

"Time," he said, simply. They'd talked of time all summer, in those few hours when Gilbert wasn't with his tutor and when Father wasn't sitting at his desk working at his accounts, or riding into town to huddle over the telephone, casting his will over place and time, trying to keep his ships and their cargos in proper and correct motion.

"Why time, Gil? You're eleven, son! You've got lots of time! You can worry about time when you're an old man."

Gilbert pretended he hadn't heard. "I was thinking of more ways that time is like space. If I was at sea, standing on the deck of a ship, I could see a certain ways before me, and if I turned around, I could see a small ways behind me. But the horizon cuts off the view in both directions. Time is like that. I can think back a certain ways, and the further back I try to remember, the fuzzier it gets, until I can't see at all. And I can see forward—we'll have cobbler soon, go to bed, wake tomorrow. But no further."

His father raised his furry eyebrows and smiled a genuine and delighted smile. "Ah, but things separated by time affect each other the way that events separated by space can't. A star dying on the other side of the universe, so far away that its light hasn't yet had time enough to crawl all the way to us, can't have any effect on us. But things that happened hundreds of years ago, like the planting of the seed that grew the oak that made this table..." He rattled his saucer on it, making his coffee sway like a rough chop. He waggled his eyebrows again.

"Yikes," Gilbert said. That hadn't occurred to him. "What if time moved in every direction and at every speed—could you have a space where events at the far end of the galaxy affected us?" He answered his own question. "Of course. Because the events could travel backwards in time—or, uh..." He fumbled, remembered Neils. "Sideways." He swallowed.

"What's sideways in time?"

He shrugged. "Sideways is sideways," he said.

His father laughed until tears rolled down his cheeks, and Gilbert didn't have the heart to tell him that the phrase had been Neils's, because making his father laugh like that was like Christmas and his birthday and a day at the beach all rolled into one.

And then his father took him down to the ocean, down the rough goat trail cut into the cliff, as surefooted as a goat himself. They watched the sun disappear behind the waves, and then they moved among the tidepools, swirling their hands in the warm, salty water to make the bioluminescent speck-size organisms light up like fireworks. They sat out and watched the moon and the stars, lying on their backs in the sand, Gilbert's head in the crook of his father's arm, and he closed his eyes and let his father tell him stories about the sea and the places he went in the long, lonely winters, while the waves went *shhh, shhh,* like the whisper of the mother who'd died giving birth to him.

Then they picked their way back up the cliff by moonlight that was so bright, it might have been day, a blue-white noon in shades of gray, and his father tucked him up into bed as if he were three years old, smoothing the covers and kissing him on the forehead with a whiskery kiss.

As he lay along a moment that stretched sleepily out like warm taffy, suspended on the edge of sleep, the thought occurred to him: *What if space moved in only one direction, in two dimensions, like time?*

The year passed. For so long as Gilbert could remember, summer's first messenger had been the postmaster, Mr. Ossinger, who rode his bicycle along the sea road to the house to deliver his father's telegram advising of his expected arrival in port and the preparations to be made for him. Mrs. Curie usually signed for the letter, then knocked on the study door to deliver it into Gilbert's eager hands.

But this year, while the wind and rain howled outside the window, and Señor Uriarte plodded through the formation of igneous rock, Mrs. Curie did not come and deliver the letter, rescuing him from geography. She didn't come to the door, though Señor had finished rocks and moved on to algebra and then to Shakespeare. Finally, the school day ended. Gilbert left Señor stirring through the coals of the study fire, adding logs against the unseasonal winds outside.

Gilbert floated downstairs to the kitchen as though trapped in a dream that compelled him to seek out the housekeeper, even though some premonition told him to hide away in his room for as long as possible.

From behind, she seemed normal, her thin shoulders working as she beat at the batter for the night's cake, cranking the mixer's handle with slow, practiced turns. But when the door clicked shut behind him, she stopped working the beater, though her shoulders kept working, shuddering, rising, falling. She turned her face to him and he let out a cry and took a step back toward the door. It was as though she had been caught by an onrush of time, one that had aged her, turning her from an old woman to an animated corpse. Every wrinkle seemed to have sunk deeper, her fine floss hair hung limp across her forehead, her eyes were red and leaked steady rills of tears.

She took a step toward him, and he wanted to turn and run, but now he was frozen. So he stood, rooted to the spot, while she came and took him up in her frail arms and clutched at him, sobbing dry, raspy sobs. "He's not coming home," she whispered into his ear, the whiskers on her chin tickling at him. "He's not coming home, Gilbert. Oh, oh, oh." He held her and patted her and the time around him seemed to crawl by, slow enough that he could visualize every sweet moment he'd had with his father, time enough to visualize every storm his father had ever narrated to him. Had all that time and more before Señor Uriarte came downstairs for his tea and found them in the kitchen. He gathered up frozen Gilbert and carried him to his bedroom, removed his shoes, and sat with him for hours until he finally slept.

When morning dawned, the storm had lifted. Gilbert went to his window to see the stupid blue sky with its awful yellow sun and realized that his father was now gone forever and ever, to the end of time.

Emmy and her brothers were queasy of him for the first week of summer, playing with him as though he were made of china or tainted with plague. But by the second week, they were back to something like normal, scampering up the trees and down the cliffs, ranging farther and farther afield on their bicycles.

Most of all, they were playing down at the switchyards, the old rail line that ran out from the disused freight docks a few miles down the beach from their houses. Señor and Mrs. Curie didn't know what to do with him that summer, lacking any direction from Father, and so Gilbert made the most of it, taking the Limburghers out on longer and longer trips, their packs bursting with food and water and useful tools: screwdrivers, crowbars, cans of oil.

Someone probably owned the switchyard, but whoever that was, he was far away and had shown no interest in it in Gilbert's lifetime. It had been decades since the freighters came into this harbor and freight trains had taken their cargos off into the land on the rusted rails. The rusted padlocks on the utility sheds crumbled and fell to bits at the lightest touch from the crowbars; the doors squealed open on their ancient hinges.

Inside, the cobwebby, musty gloom yielded a million treasures: old timetables, a telegraph rig, stiff denim coveralls with material as thick as the hall carpet at home, ancient whiskey bottles, a leather-bound journal that went to powder when they touched it, and...

A handcar.

"It'll never work," said Emmy. "That thing's older than the dinosaurs. It's practically rusted through!"

Gilbert pretended he hadn't heard her. He wished he could move the car a little closer to the grimy windows. It was almost impossible to make sense of in the deep shadows of the shed. He pushed hard on the handle, putting his weight into it. It gave a groan, a squeal, and another groan. Then it moved an inch. That was a magic inch! He got his oilcan and lavishly applied the forty-weight oil to every bearing he could find. Neils and Erwin held the lamp. Emmy leaned in closer. He pushed the handle again. Another groan, and a much higher squeal, and the handle sank under his weight. The handcar rumbled forward, almost crushing Emmy's foot—if she hadn't been so quick to leap back, she'd have been crippled. She didn't seem to mind. She, her brothers, and Gilbert were all staring at the handcar as if to say, "Where have you been all my life?"

They christened it Kalamazoo and they worked with oil and muscle until they had moved it right up to the doorway. It cut their fingers to ribbons and turned their shins into fields of bruises, but it was all worth it because of what it promised: motion without end.

The track in the switchyard went in two directions. Inland, toward the nation and its hurrying progress and its infinite hunger for materials and blood and work. And out to sea, stretching out on a rockbed across the harbor, to the breakers where the great boats that were too large for the shallow harbor used to tie up to offload. Once they had bullied Kalamazoo onto the tracks—using blocks, winches, levers, and a total disregard for their own safety—they stood to either side of its bogey handle and stared from side to side. Each knew what the others were thinking: Do we pump for the land, or pump for the sea?

"Tomorrow," Gilbert said. It was the end of August now, and lessons would soon begin again, and each day felt like something was drawing to a close. "Tomorrow," Gilbert said. "We'll decide tomorrow. Bring supplies."

That night, by unspoken agreement, they all packed their treasures. Gilbert laid out his sailor suit—his father bought him a new one every year—and his book about time and space and stuffed a picnic blanket with Mrs. Curie's preserves, hardtack bread, jars of lemonade, and apples from the cellar. Mrs. Curie—three quarters deaf—slept through his raid. Gilbert then went to his father's study and took the spyglass that had belonged to his grandfather, who had also been lost at sea. He opened the small oak box holding Grandad's sextant, but as he'd never mastered it, he set it down. He took his father's enormous silver-chased turnip watch, and tried on his rain boots and discovered that they fit. The last time he'd tried them on, he could have gotten both feet into one of them. Time had passed without his noticing, but his feet had noticed.

He hauled the bundles out to the hedgerow at the bottom of the driveway, and then he put himself to bed and in an instant he was asleep. An instant later, the sun was shining on his face. He woke, put on his sailor suit, went downstairs, and shouted hello to Mrs. Curie, who smiled a misty smile to see him in his sailor suit. She gave him hotcakes with butter and cherries from the tree behind Señor's shed, a glass of milk and a mountain of fried potatoes. He ate until his stomach wouldn't hold any more, said goodbye to her, and walked to the bottom of the hedgerow to retrieve his secret bundle. He wrestled it into his bike's basket and wobbled down to the Limburghers' gate to meet his friends, each with a bundle and a bike.

The half-hour ride to the switchyard took so little time that it was over even before Gilbert had a chance to think about what he was doing. Time was going by too fast for thoughts now, like a train that had hit its speed and could now only be perceived as a blur of passing cars and a racket of wheels and steam.

Kalamazoo was still beaded with dew as they began to unload their bundles onto its platform. Gilbert set his down at the end farthest from the sea, and Emmy set hers down at the end farthest from the land, and when they stood to either side of the pump handle, it was clear that Emmy wanted to push for the land while Gilbert wanted to push them out to sea. Naturally.

Emmy looked at Gilbert and Gilbert looked at Emmy. Gilbert took out his grandfather's spyglass, lifted off the leather cap from the business end, extended it, and pointed it out to sea, sweeping from side to side, looking farther than he'd ever seen. Wordlessly, he held it out to Emmy, who turned around to face the bay and swept it with the telescope. Then she handed it off to Neils and Erwin, who took their turns.

Nothing more had to be said. They leaned together into the stiff lever that controlled Kalamazoo's direction of travel, threw it into position, and set to pumping out to sea.

What the spyglass showed: waves and waves, and waves and waves, and, farther along, the curvature of the planet itself as it warped toward Europe and Africa and the rest of the world. It showed a spit of land, graced with an ancient and crumbling sea fort, shrouded in mist and overgrown with the weeds and trees of long disuse. And beyond it, waves and more waves.

The gentle sea breeze turned into a stiff wind once they'd pumped for an hour, the handcart at first rolling slowly on the complaining wheels. Then, as the rust flaked off the axles and the bearings found their old accommodations, they spun against one another easily. The pumping was still hard work, and even though they traded off, the children soon grew tired and sore and Emmy called for a rest stop and a snack.

As they munched their sandwiches, Gilbert had a flash. "We could use this for a sail," he said, nudging his picnic blanket with one toe. Neils and Erwin—whose shorter arms suffered more from the pumping labor—loved the idea, and set to rigging a mast from their fishing poles and the long crowbar they'd lashed to Kalamazoo's side. Emmy and Gilbert let them do the work, watching with the wisdom of age, eating sandwiches and enjoying the breeze that dried their sweat.

As they started up again, Kalamazoo seemed as refreshed from the rest as they were, and it rolled more easily than ever, the sail bellied out before the mast. When Gilbert and Emmy stopped to trade pumping duties back to the twins, Kalamazoo continued to roll, propelled by the stiff wind alone. All four children made themselves comfortable at the back of the pump car and allowed the time and the space to whip past them as they would.

"We're moving through space like time," Gilbert said.

Emmy quirked her mouth at him, a familiar no-nonsense look that he ignored.

"We are," he said. "We are moving in a straight line, from behind to in front, at a rate we can't control. Off to the sides are spaces we could move through, but we're not. We're on these rails, and we can't go sideways, can't go back, can't go up or down. We can't control our speed. We are space's slaves. This is just how we move through time."

Emmy shook her head. Neils seemed excited by the idea, though, and he nudged his twin and they muttered in their curious twinnish dialect to one another.

The sea fort was visible with the naked eye now, and with the spyglass, Gilbert could make out its brickwork and the streaks of guano that ran down its cracked walls. The rails ran right up to the fort—last used as a customs inspection point—and past it to the hidden docks on the other side of the spit.

"Better hope that the wind shifts," Emmy said, holding a wetted finger up to check the breeze.

"Otherwise we're going to have a devil of a time pumping ourselves home in time for supper."

Gilbert drew out the turnip watch, which he'd set this morning by the big grandfather clock in the front hall, carefully winding its spring. He opened its face and checked the second hand. It seemed to be spinning a little more slowly, but that could have been his imagination. According to the watch, it was nearly eleven, and they'd been on the rails for three hours.

"I think we'll make the fort in time for lunch," he said.

At the mention of food, Neils and Erwin clamored for snacks, and Emmy found them cookies she'd snitched from the big jar in the Limburgher kitchen.

Gilbert looked at the watch for a moment. The second hand had stopped moving. He held it up to his ear, and it wasn't precisely ticking any longer, but rather making a sound like a truck-wheel spinning in spring mud. He closed the lid again, and held it so tight that the intricate scrolling on the case dug into his palm.

Time passed.

And then it didn't.

And then it did again.

"Oh!" said Neils and Erwin together.

To either side of the car, stretching into infinity, were more tracks, running across the endless harbor, each with its own car, its own sail, its own children. Some were edging ahead of them. Some were going backwards. A racket overhead had them all look up at once, at the tracks there, too, the rails and the cars and the Limburghers and the Gilberts in them. Some children were older. Some were younger. One Gilbert was weeping. One was a girl.

Gilbert waved his hand, and a hundred Gilberts waved back. One made a rude gesture.

"Oh!" said Emmy. To her right, another Emmy was offering her a sandwich. She took it and handed over the last of her cookies and Emmy smiled at herself and said thank you as politely as you could wonder.

"Sideways is sideways," Neils and Erwin said together. Emmy and Gilbert nodded.

Gilbert pulled out his spyglass and looked ahead at the fort. All the rails converged on it, but without ever meeting. And some stretched beyond. And out there, somewhere, there was time like space and space like time. And somewhere there was a father on a ship that weathered a storm rather than succumbed to it.

Gilbert turned to his friends and shook each of their hands in turn. Neils was crying a little. Emmy gave Gilbert a friendly punch in the shoulder and then a hug.

There was another Kalamazoo to the right, and Gilbert was pretty sure he could easily make the leap from his car to it. And then to the next car, and the next. And beyond, into the infinite sideways.

If there was an answer, he'd find it there.

HB

Uninvited Guests

His heart was pounding.

He was sure he had seen the doorknob turn.

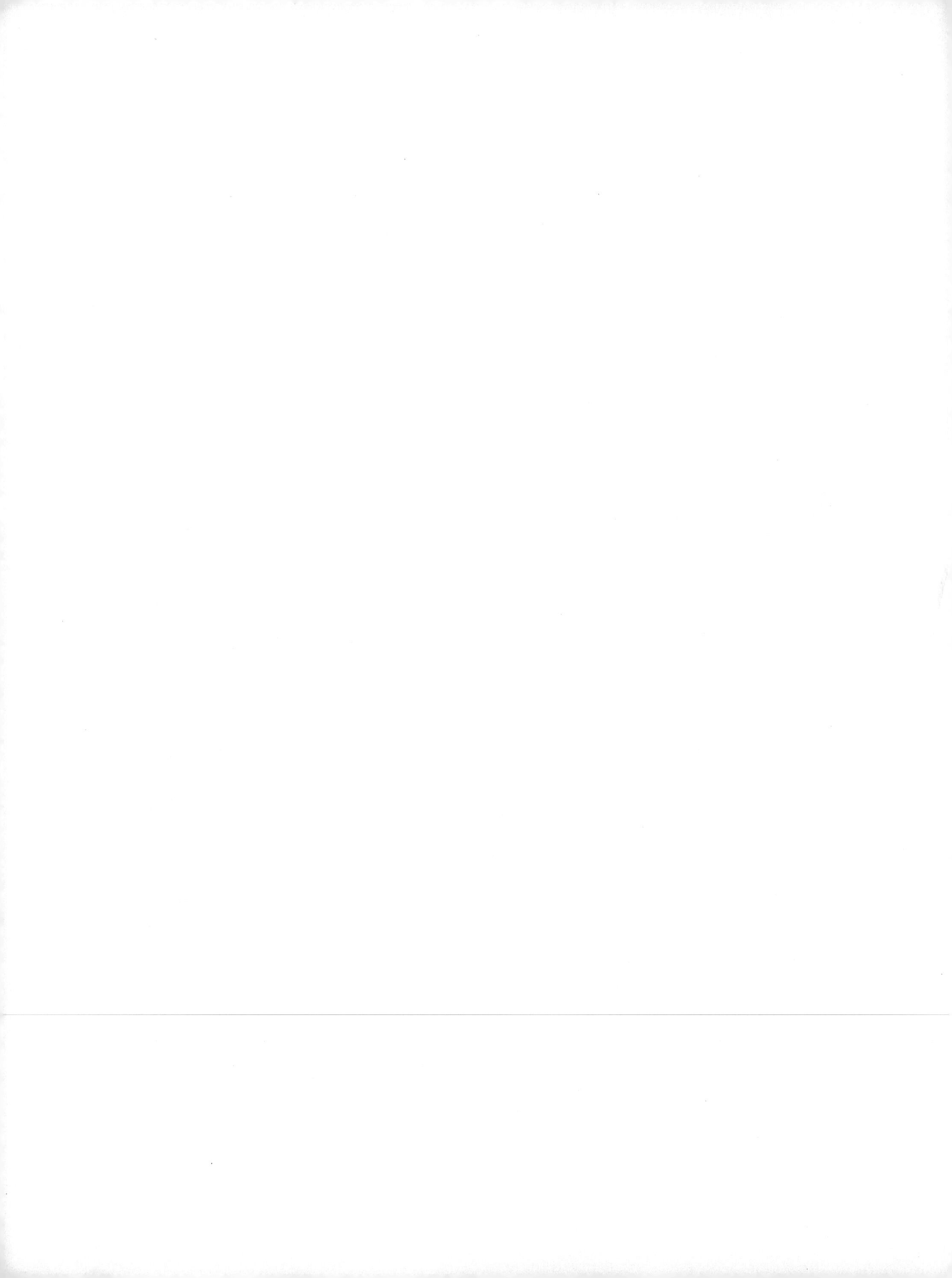

UNINVITED GUESTS

JULES FEIFFER

Henry was startled, but not that surprised by the appearance of a singing mouse in his studio. After all, he was a children's book writer and illustrator. He had been writing and drawing stories about talking and singing mice, bears, pigs, ducks, dogs, cats, mules, donkeys, elephants, foxes, sharks, whales, eagles, and owls, as well as chattering flowers, chairs, tables, and once an entire avenue of three-bedroom houses that wouldn't keep still.

It was his own three-bedroom house in which the singing mouse displayed itself to Henry. The event occurred sometime after his wife had taken his two boys off on vacation—a vacation that had now lasted over a year—complaining that she could no longer stand living in this house, stacked with children's paraphernalia long after their own two boys had reached adolescence, cramped with odds and ends that began as research for his picture books and ended up as living room décor, bedroom flotsam, kitchen gewgaws, and bathroom clutter. Building blocks of all colors rising to the ceiling, toy cars of different makes and sizes, three sets of toy trains, crossing back and forth in all of the upstairs rooms: bedrooms, bathrooms, and Henry's studio. Stuffed animals, including a life-size elephant, a hippopotamus, a camel, and a zebra. Stuffed life-size dolls based on animal characters that Henry had created so many years ago, he couldn't remember their names. And most irritating of all to his wife, Wilma, the artifact that drove her to leave the house and never return until Henry did something about it (which he refused to do), was the 150-foot-long boa constrictor, so real-looking that it frightened his wife and disturbed the dreams of his teenage boys. The snake, four inches in diameter and dyed in incandescent colors, ran from Henry's studio upstairs, downstairs into the living room, across to the kitchen, and down into the cellar, where its head came to rest against a tiny oak door in the stone basement wall that Henry had tried but had never been able to open. Behind the door, Henry smelled chicken soup.

His wife's last act before driving off with the children was to take the ax Henry used to chop firewood and make piecemeal out of all 150 feet of stuffed boa constrictor, from its head in the basement cellar to its tail in Henry's studio. Then she gathered her sons in the family station wagon and took off on their permanent vacation.

Henry regretted their departure, but not quite as much as the passing of his favorite boa—who now, fifteen months after his dismemberment—reappeared whole again, in fine fettle, curled comfily around the talking mouse, the two of them singing an off-key but exuberant version of "Puff the Magic Dragon."

Henry viewed this apparition with equanimity. He had been living inside his head for so long that he was comfortable with the ridiculous and completely at ease with the absurd. Incoherence shaped the day-to-day state of his mind, a fact of life that had upset his family but felt absolutely right to Henry.

He loved what didn't fit, didn't make sense, wasn't efficient, structured, or orderly. He distrusted order. His mind was a mess, his graying hair uncut and uncombed, a messy growth that hid a messier mind. His implausible brain delighted in the unlikely sight and sound that had taken up residence in his studio: these two creatures, a perfect match for the imaginings of a children's book author and illustrator, who were harmonizing favorite songs from Henry's childhood, moving on from "Puff the Magic Dragon" to "Zip-a-Dee-Doo-Dah" and then to "Rudolph the Red-Nosed Reindeer."

"Who are you?" Henry demanded, and then corrected himself. "I know very well who you are: Monte the Mouse from my first book, *The Mouse Who Ate Caviar,* and Bobo the Boa from *Mr. Snake Goes to Town,* one of my worst books, maybe one of the worst picture books ever written. Why have you come back to sing for me? What is it you are trying to convey by singing my childhood favorites? Are you going to sing 'Heigh-ho, Heigh-ho, it's off to work we go'? Please, don't! Is there some hidden meaning to your weird and mysterious appearance? A *message,* perhaps? Please tell me you didn't come here with a message! I despise messages! I have never written a book with a message. My whole life has been in pursuit of an existence without messages, without well-meaning advice, without improving my mind, without meeting and fleeing from that which is good for me, will change me for the better, convert me, inspire me. I wish for nothing but to be left to myself and my characters, of which you are two, but certainly not my most successful two. What does it mean? Wait, I take it back! I don't want to know what anything means! I only care about silliness, goofiness, slapstick, and childhood before the age of seven and a half. And I smell smoke! Why do I smell smoke? Is that another illusion?"

But no! Sadly not. Henry looked away from the singing mouse and boa to see that his studio had caught fire. The candle he lit every morning at seven a.m. when he entered his studio to work, the candle that set his mood to his happy past—the games and play and running around he remembered from childhood—that burning candle had somehow come in contact with sketches Henry had tossed aside earlier. Apparently he'd tossed them into the lit candle, which ignited the sketch paper and set his studio on fire. Henry might have noticed the fire early enough to do something about it, except for the distraction of the singing mouse and boa constrictor, who were now leading him out of the smoke-filled studio as they sang and danced their way downstairs to "Row, row, row your boat, gently down the stream."

Henry could not see that well anymore—the smoke was thick, the smell was sickening—and he could not think (well, he could never think). He didn't try to call for help or contain the fire; he didn't believe that to be appropriate behavior. What he deemed appropriate was to follow the singing and dancing creatures of his own invention to wherever they led him.

And why not? He had spent half a lifetime directing creatures he had made up into hapless and hilarious situations. Why shouldn't they turn the tables? And what better time than now? He was old, and getting older by the minute, and had been abandoned by his family. (Or had he abandoned them? Now was not the time to resolve the question.)

Because now Henry's universe was burning! Like Henry's picture book of fifteen years ago, *The Firehouse Fire,* in which feckless firefighters (dogs and cats) got in one another's way as they battled the blaze that would have consumed their firehouse if not for the good luck of a sudden monsoon that flooded the premises. The firehouse sailed away in a gumbo of helplessly confused fireanimals.

But no monsoon was on the way to save Henry's house. It was about to burn to the ground with Henry in it, unless this mouse and boa had a plan. Henry had no plan, not a single thought in his head, except to follow the singing animals that he had given life to, and on whom he was now depending for his rescue.

As the mouse hopped and the boa slithered downstairs to the main floor, they waded into a rousing chorus of "Come on, baby, light my fire."

Henry didn't hear, wasn't listening. None of this was to his liking. He had moved into this house specifically to avoid the intrusion of life into fantasy. Over the years he had endured more than enough forced and unwanted choices, heaped upon more unwanted choices, leading to even more unintended, unwanted choices. Now he was finished with choices. Except what story to tell, what animal to focus on, what twist of overworked, long-favored surprise endings to spring on his young readers? And after that, what brush to apply with which color to what quality of paper. His work—that, and that alone—had become his life.

So he was in no mind to deal with a house burning down around him. If choices had to be made, Henry trusted the mouse and the boa to make them.

But where were they all headed now? As the smoke thickened and began to trail Henry, the mouse, and the boa downstairs, the cellar door swung open and down into its dark, cool depths Henry descended. No smoke yet. In fact, cool, still calmly cool, as if in defiance of all that was burning above. The cellar door blew shut behind Henry and his creatures, leaving them in darkness. A single shaft of light eased only slightly Henry's wariness of the darkened, hulking shapes and forbidding silhouettes that were everywhere before him. In the far wall, lit by the glow cast from the window, Henry was able to make out the tiny door that he had never been able to pry open. It was toward this door that he saw the mouse and the boa heading. And then they were at the door . . . and gone. Through, under, or over the door? "Wait!" cried Henry. "What do I do now?"

A voice behind the door yelled, "Is that you, Henry?" He recognized it immediately. It was the voice of Lena the Lioness, the way she sounded in his imagination when he wrote and drew his bestseller, *A Lioness in Summer.*

"Well, I must say it took you long enough!" came a second voice, familiar from the months spent making up lines inside his head. It was Wesley Worm, the hero of his popular picture book *The Worm Returns.*

All of these voices, dozens now jabbering, mixed with animal sounds: oinking, quacking, barking, meowing, honking, mooing... an entire menagerie shouted as they quacked and meowed and mooed: "Henry!" "It's Henry!" "About time, Henry!"

Henry coughed. Smoke had begun to seep in from upstairs. It curled under the cellar door. But it was that other door, the tiny mystery door, that held Henry's attention. It seemed to grow brighter as the smoke advanced. "Good heavens!" Henry said aloud. "There's a message here!" He clapped his hands at the joy of self-discovery. "What I've tried to avoid my entire working life—and look what I've done!"

He took a further careful step downstairs. "I've set a trap for myself, and I'm walking right into it!" He clapped his hands twice now, as if in applause for the conclusion he was reaching. "I made this whole thing up to conceal the obvious: that I am dying. I have constructed a clever little story, laced with all my skills of fantasy and misdirection, to bring me to this door and to deliver the message that I could not accept in any other form. I have turned my death into a children's story. Oh, I am a much better writer than I ever imagined!"

Feeling an excitement he hadn't known since he was a little boy, Henry descended the last of the steps, nervously advancing toward his port of entry. His heart was pounding. He was sure he had seen the doorknob turn.

HB

The Harp

So it's true, he thought, it's really true.

THE HARP

LINDA SUE PARK

The old magician took off his cape slowly.

He had earned it, the ancient green cape bestowed on him in gratitude for his life's work. There was a scroll as well, inscribed with real gold leaf. *For distinguished service to humankind.*

It hadn't been easy, serving humankind in the late twentieth and early twenty-first centuries. The problems in every corner of the world had been endless and at times seemingly insurmountable. But the hardest part of his job was that very few people believed in magic anymore.

Which meant that he and his colleagues could not perform the sweeping dramatic acts that had made magicians, witches, wizards, mages, seers, and shamans renowned and revered over the millennia of human existence. These days, they would be laughed at as charlatans or crackpots. Or worse.

Instead, they had to work in secret and with stealth. Good timing, coincidence, serendipity: the tools of the modern magician's trade. The rain that doused a spark before it became a forest fire. A better-than-average harvest. A long-lost friend found via an Internet search for kumquats. There had been times when he longed to put together something a bit more dramatic, but he had stifled that desire for the greater good.

Now he would retire for a well-earned rest, and work perhaps just a little magic closer to home.

Emma and Frances were taking one of their bicker walks in the woods not far from their home. They went for bicker walks regularly—several times a week, in fact. The sisters bickered constantly, the full range from snide twits to wide-open, full-throttle arguments. Especially in the summer, when they were home together for long hours. Whenever one parent or the other got tired of hearing them, they were told, TAKE YOURSELVES AND YOUR BICKERING OUT OF THE HOUSE THIS INSTANT.

Today, by the time the girls reached the path into the woods, they had completely forgotten the cause of this particular walk, having already embarked on a new bicker.

"I get the first one."

"Why should you get it? I want it just as much as you do."

"I want it more."

"No, *I* want it more."

"How do you know how much I want it? You think you know everything."

They were arguing about who got to pick the first blackberry. But it was only June, too early for blackberries, which meant that they were bickering over something that didn't even exist yet.

Emma was almost twelve and would be in sixth grade in the fall. Before this particular walk, she would have said that she didn't believe in magic. Frances, two years younger, would have said she wasn't sure.

One minute they were ambling toward a stand of brambles; the next they were in a cave. A man stood before them with a harp at his side.

Emma blinked several times. *This can't be happening,* she thought. And then: *What a clichéd thing to think. But anyway, it must be a dream, so I'll go with it for now.*

Except for his sudden presence, there was nothing terribly frightening about the man. He was rather ordinary-looking—medium height, with a tanned complexion, gray hair, and dark eyes—the only unusual thing about him being his cape. It had some fraying around the edges, but was a cheerful green hue, between lime and emerald. Emma thought a black cape might have been scarier, if scary was the effect he was going for.

It took him only moments to cast the spell, which he did by whirling the cape around his body and over his head several times. Frances made a noise of admiration, and Emma sensed that her sister was longing to try cape-whirling herself. Then the magician handed Emma a scroll and vanished, having said not a word.

Emma immediately began reading aloud from the parchment:

- *The spell will be broken when Frances learns to play the harp well enough to satisfy the conditions set by the writer William Congreve, who wrote: "Music hath charms to soothe a savage breast, to soften rocks, or bend a knotted oak."*
- *You are permitted to leave the cave as necessary, but do not attempt to leave the woods.*
- *You are in a bubble of time. Your family will not miss you: Time will pass much more slowly for them than for you.*

"Emma?"

It was Frances's voice, but it came from the ground near Emma's feet. Emma looked down and let out a screech of horror.

Frances had been turned into a frog.

Emma screeched a few more times and hyperventilated. Frances hopped madly around the cave.

After this reasonable interval of panic, the sisters (*If your sister has been turned into a frog, she's still your sister, isn't she?*) decided together that neither of them was dreaming. They calmed down, doing their best to think brave thoughts. Emma: *I have to figure this out and take care of Frances.* Frances: *I've always been the adventurous one. I have to keep my head here, or else Emma will really freak out.*

Their first plan was to try to leave the woods, Emma carrying Frances in the palm of her hand. They smacked right into an invisible barrier, like a force field in science-fiction movies. After some exploration, they determined that the barrier had a rough circumference of perhaps a hundred yards, with the stream marking part of it—which Frances discovered by jumping in from one bank and trying to jump out the other side.

Wham into the force field, *splash* back into the stream.

Escape thus stymied, the sisters turned to the other terms of the spell. Emma was in her second year of violin lessons, but a violin was very different from a harp. She had never even seen a harp up close. Still, she knew more about music than Frances did.

Frances had never played a musical instrument. She had just finished third grade and would not begin music lessons until fourth.

Besides which, she was now a frog.

"No! I won't go! You can't make me!" Brian slammed his bedroom door, then kicked it a few times.

What he'd said wasn't true. Dad could indeed make him stay with Gramps for the summer.

Mom would at least have listened. She had always done her best to treat him like a sixth-grader, not a baby. But she probably would have sided with Dad in the end, and then Brian would have been mad at both of them.

No, that didn't make any sense either. If Mom were still alive, there wouldn't be any talk about Brian living with Gramps all summer.

Gramps had brought up the idea at Mom's funeral in February.

"It'll do you good," Gramps said.

"How could living in the middle of nowhere do me any good?" Brian yelled. Right there in the funeral home. Everyone stared, then turned away uneasily.

Brian stormed out of the building. Unable to think of what else to do, he sat in the car and missed the whole service. Missed his chance to say a last goodbye to Mom.

A whole summer where he didn't know anyone, miles away from anything to do. It was typical of the way his life was going these days. He had gotten in trouble at school several times for cutting classes. He'd quit playing soccer right before he would have gotten kicked off the team for yelling at everyone—the refs and the opponents and his teammates too. He had driven away his friends one by one with his angry outbursts and overall surliness.

And Dad thought Brian spent too much time on the computer or playing video games. Dad was always nagging at him to get outside, ride his bike, *do* something.

Gramps didn't have a computer or a game system. He didn't even have a television.

"Radio and good books," Gramps always said. "Don't need more than that."

It was going to be the worst summer of Brian's life.

Gramps himself was okay, as grownups went. Brian didn't really know him all that well. He didn't talk much and neither did Brian, which seemed to suit both of them. And things began to look up a little the day after Brian's dad left to go back to the city.

"Thought we'd go to the animal shelter," Gramps said at the breakfast table. "Been meaning to get a dog. Now's as good a time as any."

Brian sat up straight for the first time in months. He had always wanted a dog, but pets weren't allowed in the apartment where he and Dad lived.

"It'll have to stay here when you go back," Gramps said.

Of course. No good news without bad to go with it.

There were fifteen dogs in the shelter. All of them were sort of something—sort of spaniel, sort of retriever, sort of terrier. Each dog nosed through the bars of its cage and wagged its tail when Brian approached. How was he ever going to choose?

Three times he went around the crates—and was no closer to a decision than when he began. At one point Brian looked up to see every single dog staring at him, and he could have sworn they all had hope in their eyes.

Brian felt confusion first, followed by the familiar warmth of anger stirring inside him. *I thought this would be fun! But now I don't know what to do—I can't pick one over another. I hate this!*

"This is stupid," he said to Gramps. "It's gonna be your dog—you should choose."

Gramps gazed at him steadily. "I don't care. You pick."

Brian turned away, glaring at the floor. He hated when people said that—*I don't care*—it always made him want to shout, "CARE! WHY DON'T

YOU CARE?" It seemed like there were so many things people didn't care about. Like all these dogs...

An idea hit him.

A really good idea.

"The dogs," he said to the volunteer, "out of all of them, which one is—I mean, is there one who... whose time is almost up?"

The woman pointed without hesitation. "That one," she said. "He's been here for almost a month."

A tan and gray dog—white face, pointed ears and snout. A sort-of husky.

"He came in off the street, no tags," the woman said. "That means you get to name him whatever you want."

She opened the cage and the dog trotted right to Brian. He knelt down and scratched it behind the ears.

"Hey there," Brian said softly. "Wanna come home with us?"

The dog whined a little and wagged his tail. He looked at Brian as if trying to tell him something.

"Douglas," Brian said. The name had popped into his head out of the blue.

He looked up at Gramps; it would be Gramps's dog after Brian left. "Is that okay?"

"Douglas," Gramps said slowly, as if he were tasting the name. Then a little louder: "Douglas?"

The dog turned his head to look at Gramps.

"He already knows his name," the volunteer said with a grin. "You could call him Dougie for short, maybe."

Brian wanted to point out that Dougie was hardly any shorter than Douglas, but he decided not to. She was only trying to be nice.

And not five minutes after they got back to Gramps's place, it turned out that Dougie was a pretty good name after all. Because after the dog marked the whole back yard, he started to dig.

He dug, and dug, and dug.

Dougie.

On the very first day of harp practice, Frances pointed out the obvious.

"I can't play the normal way," she said. "My arms—er, my front legs aren't long enough to get at the strings from both sides."

She plucked at the bottom of one string, which gave out a dismal twang, then hopped up on the frame and stretched for the higher strings.

"This is impossible," she complained. "I can't even reach all of them."

After some discussion, the sisters decided that nothing in the rules barred Emma from helping Frances. After all, it was Emma who had carried the harp out of the cave and placed it on a flat rock next to the stream so Frances could have easy access to the water when she wanted a quick dip or a drink.

"Gotta stay hydrated," Frances said, exercising her newly acquired frog instincts.

And of course, Emma needed to teach Frances the basics of music.

Now she picked Frances up and stood next to the harp.

"Look," Emma said. "I can hold my hands like this"—she spread them about eight inches apart—"and you can hop from one to the other, and I can move them to put you wherever you want to be."

This strategy enabled Frances to reach all the strings. The next task was to figure out how she could elicit a true note from the harp. It required delicate maneuvering for Frances to pluck a string with a webbed toe. She also found it difficult to keep her throat from puffing out. When her throat touched a vibrating string, not only did the sound die, but her whole head twangled and twizzered.

"Put me down," Frances said at the end of the first day. She flopped on the ground, exhausted. "I've never been so tired in my whole life. Will you catch me some flies, please? The bluey-green ones are the nicest."

"Yuck," Emma said. "Catch your own flies."

Cue noisy bickering, which lasted until Frances splashed off in a huff.

After a week, Frances could pluck out a recognizable rendition of "Twinkle, Twinkle, Little Star"—and Emma was so sick of hearing it that she had to remind herself not to clench her fists. Frances might not be able to land easily on a fist and might fall; in the worst-case bad-timing scenario, Emma could end up with a handful of squashed frog-sister. So she gritted her teeth instead.

"But it doesn't sound like a harp," Frances said. "It just sounds like plucking. Harp music, it should have parts where, you know, you play a whole bunch of the strings fast, so it sounds like—like a waterfall or something."

"Glissando," Emma said. "You're right." For the next several days, the sisters developed and practiced a glissando technique. It involved Frances extending one toe to rake over the strings while Emma moved her hand back and forth.

Glissandos were hard on poor Frances. Her whole body juddered bone-shakingly each time. She developed blisters on her toes, and the webs of her feet got all stretched out.

"It's all right for you," Frances grumbled. "You're not a frog."

Emma had no answer to that.

Dougie's enthusiasm for digging seemed boundless. But he wouldn't dig just anywhere. He would trot around, sniff here and there, paw at the ground a little, and often reject a spot, followed by more trotting and sniffing. He left behind a landscape comprising holes of various sizes, mounds of grass and leaves mixed with soil, and patches of plowed-up earth. Gramps's yard both front and back looked like the site of a major archaeological dig.

A few days after Dougie came to live with them, Gramps got fed up. "Don't want him digging up the yard anymore," he said. "Take that dog into the woods, let him dig there."

Brian scowled and pressed his lips together. It felt like Gramps was kicking Dougie out of the yard, just like Dad had kicked Brian out of the apartment.

Gramps gave Brian a quick look, as if he knew what Brian was thinking. "While you're out there, you might try listening for the music."

"What music?"

"Woods music," Gramps said.

Brian stared in surprise. That was weird, coming from Gramps. Too—too poetic, or something.

Gramps had already taken Brian on a couple of walks through the woods. He showed Brian where the main paths were, and how the stream would lead him to the road if he ever got lost. Gramps seemed to know everything about the woods, but as usual, he didn't talk much on their walks. Which was fine with Brian. He wanted to discover the woods himself.

On entering the woods with Dougie, Brian had to smile at the dog's response. Dougie was practically beside himself with joy—sniffing madly at everything, bounding through the trees ahead of Brian, coming back to his side, bounding away again.

Brian lost sight of Dougie for a few moments, then caught up with him at a big old oak tree. The tree had apparently passed the Dougie sniff test, because now the dog was digging happily at its base. He paused and barked a few times.

"What is it, Dougie-boy?" Brian squatted down, but Dougie barked again, looking up at the tree's broad branches.

Brian frowned. "Is there something up there? You want me to go see?"

The old oak was that rarest of specimens: a perfect climbing tree. In just a few minutes, Brian was up amid the branches, seeing the woods from a whole new angle. The lower limbs were broad enough to sit on comfortably, and Brian immediately began making plans. *I could bring lunch . . . and a book . . .*

Dougie dug contentedly at the base of the tree while Brian made his plans in the branches. *Maybe even build a tree house, or at least some kind of platform. A basket with a rope so I could haul Dougie up . . .*

As Brian was getting ready to climb back down, he froze and lifted his head like a deer on alert.

Was that . . . *music?*

Brian frowned, listening hard. Perhaps he had imagined it. Or it could have been something else, like a bird . . .

No, not a bird. It had definitely sounded like some kind of musical instrument—a guitar, or something with strings, anyway.

He heard it again, and this time he was sure. Not really a tune, but a whole bunch of notes all blurring together, as if someone was running a finger over the strings of—of whatever it was. The music was coming from deeper in the woods. *If I got up higher, maybe I could see . . .*

Brian climbed quickly. He got more than halfway up the tree; the branches weren't nearly as broad here. Holding on to a branch over his head, he scooted sideways out onto a limb, trying to find a clear line of sight through the trees.

He focused hard on the music. It was so faint that at times he could barely hear it. Then it would get a tiny bit louder, and at those moments he thought he almost recognized a tune. *The ABC Song? Or maybe "Twinkle, Twinkle, Little Star"? Wait—it could be "Baa Baa Black Sheep"... Never noticed it before, but they all have almost the same tune...*

Brian was concentrating so hard on listening that he didn't notice he was leaning toward the sound. Bit by imperceptible bit, his feet shifted. The branch began to sag under Brian's weight. With each tiny movement he made, it bent a little more.

Brian was now singing softly, trying to fit the words to the tune:

"H-I, J-K, L-M-N-O—YIKES!"

The bent bough snapped. Brian fell, twigs scratching him and leaves whipping into his eyes; he prayed that he would break an arm or a leg, not his neck.

He landed, rolled, and sat up in astonishment.

No crack of broken bones. No pain at all, in fact.

Just Dougie's warm breath and wet tongue greeting him.

Brian had fallen into a large soft mound of dirt and leaf mold. Beside the pile was a big hole.

Dougie had done his thing again.

Frances was finally proficient at "Twinkle, Twinkle" and could even throw in a decent glissando or two. The sisters were now trying to satisfy the musical standards of the spell.

"Okay, so we've got to 'soothe a savage beast, soften rocks or bend a knotted oak,'" Emma said, quoting the parchment.

"Do you think we have to do all three? Or just one of them?"

"It says 'or,'," Emma pointed out, "but we should probably try to do all of them."

"Just to be safe," Frances agreed.

There were lots of squirrels in the woods and many birds, too. Emma had seen a deer a couple of times, and a raccoon at the stream one evening.

"I don't think you could call any of those 'savage,'" she said.

"Are there bears?" Frances asked. "Bears would definitely count as savage."

"I've never heard of bears out here," Emma said, "and besides, there is no way in this lifetime that I'm going to hold you while you try to soothe a rampaging bear by playing 'Twinkle Twinkle.'"

"Minnows," Frances proposed. "I've seen lots of minnows in the stream. Maybe some of them are baby piranhas. Do you think *potentially* savage beasts count?"

Emma wasn't sure if potential counted, and she was even less sure that the minnows were piranhas. They tried anyway: Emma threw a handful of crumbs into the water (bread, cheese, and fruit appeared nightly in the cave for her—nourishing and tasty, albeit monotonous) to draw the minnows close. Frances plucked away, but the minnows continued their usual darting and twitching and did not seem the least bit soothed.

The sisters then decided that, in the interest of safety, attempts to soothe any other beasts should be last on their list. They tried rock-softening next.

"You know how if you sing a really high note you can shatter a glass?" Frances said hopefully. "Maybe it works like that."

Emma fetched rocks of assorted sizes and types and lined them up next to the harp. Frances played her heart out.

Nothing happened. The rocks were utterly unperturbed by "Twinkle, Twinkle," with or without glissandos. After a few fruitless hours, Emma swept the rocks away and replaced them with a variety of sticks from a nearby oak tree. Together the sisters went through several dozen more repetitions of the song.

"Anything?" Frances panted, her throat swelling.

Emma set Frances down on the rock. She picked up a stick and examined it closely. "Maybe," she said slowly. "I think—I'm not sure—it could be a *tiny* bit more bent than it was before? Let's keep going, just a little longer..."

"It's no use," Frances said at last, in both exhaustion and despair. She hopped into the stream to refresh herself.

Emma flung away the stick she was holding. As she walked back to the cave, she felt her resolve crumbling. There was no way harp music could soften a rock or bend a piece of wood. Did that mean...Would they be stuck here forever?

And poor Frances—would she be a frog for the rest of her life?

In the distance, Brian could see a girl with her back to him. She was standing next to the stream, playing a harp. All he could really see was that she had dark curly hair.

Since he had first heard the music, Brian had spent a lot of time in the woods, trying to trace its source. With Dougie at his side, he had tramped over what seemed like every inch of the woods. But he hadn't heard the music again all summer.

Instead, he heard other things. Birdsong. Rain pattering on the leaves.

The sigh of the wind in the upper branches. The rustles and buzzes of hundreds of tiny creatures going about their lives. The near-silence that was full of life.

He'd heard the real music of the woods. And he liked it so much, he stopped feeling compelled to find that other music.

Now, when he wasn't looking for it, here it was again.

The girl was downstream from him, and on the far side. Brian stayed put; he felt that if he moved too close or tried to call out to her, she would simply disappear. It didn't feel like a silly thought. Maybe it was his imagination, but there definitely seemed to be something weird and otherworldly in the air. Weird, but not scary.

Brian eased himself down onto a rock. It was rough-surfaced and uneven, not the most comfortable seat. Dougie sat beside him, and Brian curled his fingers into the soft fur on the dog's nape.

Brian wasn't a musician himself, or he might have noticed that the girl was in the wrong position to play a harp—facing the strings rather than astride its frame. And he was too far away to see that she wasn't actually even touching the strings.

But he could hear the music. The ABC song—or maybe "Twinkle, Twinkle"—as he had never heard it before. It was as if the harp and the stream were playing together—plinks and splashes, ripples and waves, water and notes in perfect counterpoint.

Harp music. Stream music. Woods music. They all came together, and Brian found himself thinking of Gramps, and his dad, and then his mom, and soon tears were sliding down his cheeks and Dougie was nudging closer to comfort him.

Brian had no idea how long he sat there crying quietly, oblivious to the cold, hard rock beneath him. The harp music ended. Still in a daze, he didn't notice when the girl disappeared among the trees. Nor did he hear the tiny plop of a frog diving into the stream.

Brian hugged Dougie, stood up slowly, and took one last look at the harp.

So it's true, he thought, *it's really true. Woods music . . .*

"Come on, Dougie," he said aloud. "Time to go home."

The next morning, Emma woke in the cave to see Frances still asleep next to her.

Frances the person, not Frances the frog.

Emma whooped and woke her sister, who in her first dazed and confused moments hopped on all fours several times before readjusting to her two feet.

"WE DID IT! WE DID IT!" Emma crowed.

"But—but how?" Frances said even as she hugged her sister in excitement. "We didn't soften the rocks, or bend any of that wood. Or soothe a savage beast either—I don't get it—"

Emma grabbed the parchment, which they had kept rolled up under a rock.

"Where does it say—oh, right here . . . 'music to soothe—the savage BREAST'!" she shouted. "Not *beast!* We read it wrong!"

Frances was still puzzled. "So we soothed someone's breast?"

Emma rolled her eyes but was too excited to bicker. "I'm sure it means, like, their heart. Their feelings, you know?" Then she frowned. "But you're right. Who—"

"The boy!" Frances exclaimed.

"What boy?"

"Last night, when I hopped out of the stream, I saw a boy. He was sitting on a rock, crying, and I was just about to come and get you, but then he went away."

"He was crying? Doesn't seem like the music soothed him," Emma said doubtfully.

"No, it was him, all right." Frances was sure of it. "A good cry can be very soothing." She herself had experienced a number of prolonged crying sessions—usually the result of particularly fierce bickers—and always felt much better afterwards.

Emma looked at her sister with new respect. "It was really you," she said. "You did the hard part."

Frances blushed in pleasure and surprise. "But I never could have done it without you," she said.

"Indeed," said a voice from outside the cave entrance. "And don't feel too bad about your mistake with Congreve. Lots of folks do the same; it's one of the most misquoted lines in English literature."

Together the girls ran outside, but they were too late. All they saw was a last whirl of bright green cape disappearing into thin air.

"House is too big for me on my own anyway," Gramps said.

"It'll be good to be all together," Dad said. "A bachelor pad." He smiled and clapped Brian on the back.

Brian could hardly believe his ears. They were moving out of the city, and in with Gramps.

He'd get to stay with Dougie. And the woods.

For a few days, things were all jumble and fluster as Brian and Dad moved their stuff into Gramps's house. Dad sent Brian to the attic to store some boxes. Everything up there was generously furred with dust, and Brian sneezed a few times.

There was a heap of old worn-out clothes nearby. Brian wiped the snot from his hand on whatever was on top.

Some old green thing that probably hadn't been used in years.

HB

Mr. Linden's Library

He had warned her about the book.

Now it was too late.

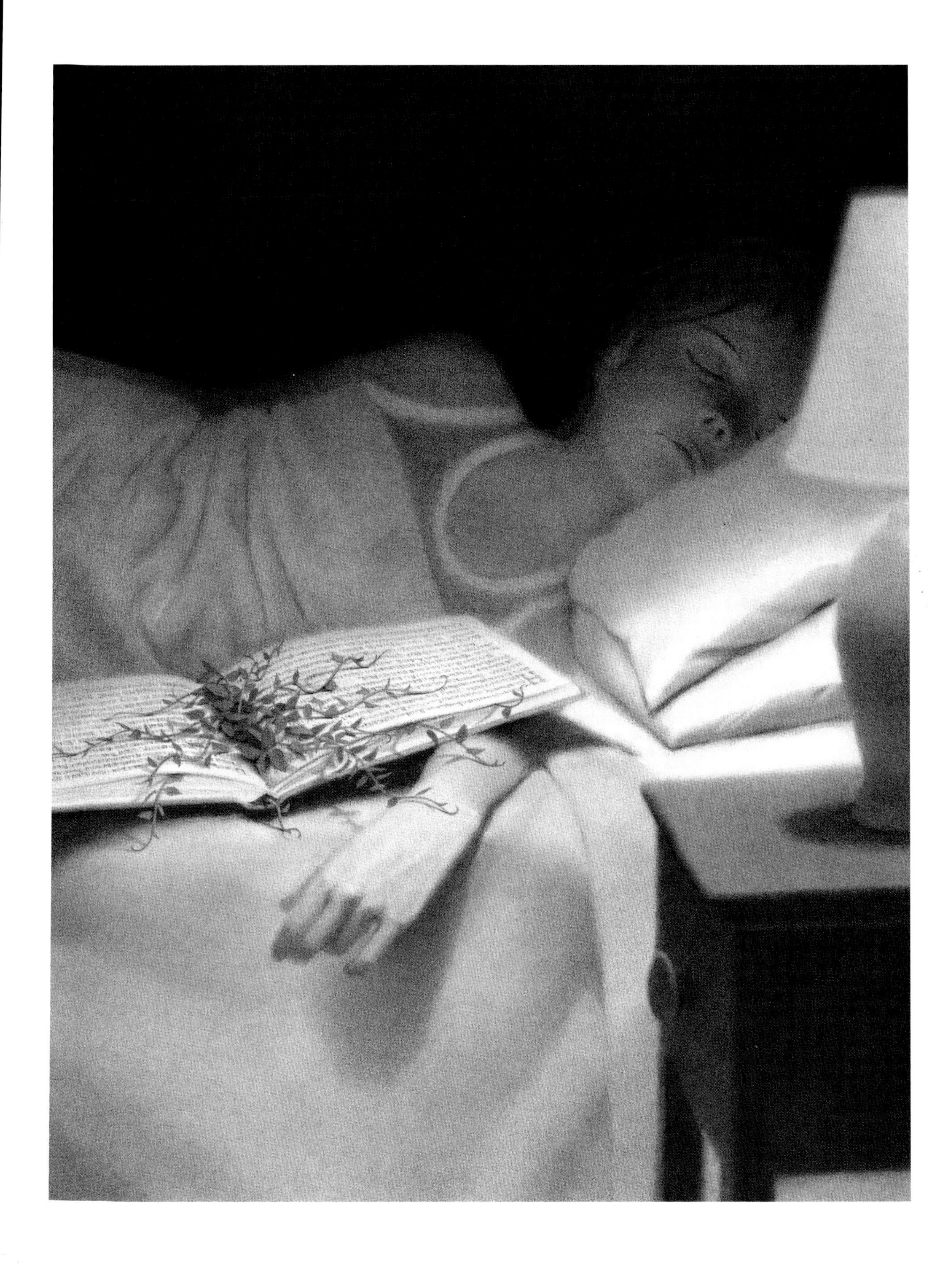

MR. LINDEN'S LIBRARY

WALTER DEAN MYERS

You wouldn't see anything special about Josiah Linden's house if you passed it on the road, which ran from town up to the small bluff that overlooked Allen's Bay. A scrawny oak tree, gnarled and twisted from years of catching the wind off the bay, sat in front, spoiling what symmetry the old house ever had. The back side of the house looked fairly formidable, especially the rounded corner that seemed for all the world like the turret of a small castle. There were some nights, however, when the moon was full or nearly so, that the corner of the house would glow white against the darkness of the trees and shrubbery behind it and take on an eerie glow.

Carol Jenkins didn't know much about Mr. Linden, except that he was one of the few black people in that area of Nova Scotia. The story about him, mostly gathered from the lips of people curious about the old man, or from American Revolutionary War buffs who knew that his ancestors could have been among the ex-slaves who had sided with British, was that Mr. Linden had been a merchant seaman most of his life. He wasn't a big man, and when he walked he shifted his weight more from side to side than straight forward. He was lively, though, and always had a smile for whoever was passing, and a slight wave of the hand. The first time Carol remembered having seen Mr. Linden was in the hardware store, talking to a group of young men about weather conditions in the Arctic.

"The cold can catch you when you're not even thinking about it. It caught me about thirty years ago and I lost a bit of my finger to frostbite," he had said, holding up his hand so that the small crowd could see where the tip of the second finger of his left hand had been amputated.

"You must have been all over the world," one of the onlookers had remarked.

"The lure of seeing new places, different ways of life, has been almost irresistible," Mr. Linden had replied. "Now I collect stories about those places. Pictures and books about the places I've been and places I'd still like to go someday. I have more than two thousand books in my collection."

Carol mentioned this story to her friend Peter, who dismissed the idea at once.

"John Altman was up to his place doing some repairs on the window frames, and he said it looked like the old guy read the same page of the same book every day. I bet he doesn't even know how to read."

Carol didn't believe Peter but decided not to make a big deal of it, and the matter would have gone completely from her mind if she and her mother hadn't run into Mr. Linden the following April.

It was one of those days that the wind, swirling relentlessly from the north, found every opening a poorly buttoned coat offered up and rattled the windows of Brendel's General Store ominously against their frames. Mr. Linden was waiting while the clerk measured out a pound of coffee beans.

"Just the thought of a good hot cup of coffee makes me feel warmer," he said in the direction of Carol and her mother.

"Mr. Linden, do you think I could borrow one of your books one day?" Carol's request surprised even her.

Mr. Linden looked toward Carol's mother, his brows arched questioningly.

"Oh, that would be too much of a bother to you, sir," her mother said quickly.

"Books are meant to be read," Mr. Linden said. "If you bring the young lady around she can have her pick. I'm sure she'll be careful with them."

The Glace Bay Library was small and didn't carry many of the adventure books that Carol liked. After she promised her mother that she did really want to expand her reading and would absolutely take care of the books, Carol and her mother made the short trek up the hill to Mr. Linden's house on a Wednesday afternoon.

The interior of Mr. Linden's home was bright with sunlight that streamed through the starched patterned curtains. In the library itself there were dark green bookcases along the wall, and a small writing desk was in the middle of the rectangular room. The surface of the writing desk was covered with dark leather, and in one corner there was a wooden box that contained a sextant. The window seat that looked out over the bay was just wide enough to sit in and, if you were a twelve-year-old girl with a small frame, put your feet up as you read.

"You must really love books," Carol said when she saw just how many books the old sailor had.

"Books have always been among my most trusted of friends," Mr. Linden replied. "The best of them allow the mind to wander wherever the author's musings lead. I'm reading the book that's lying there, but the rest are yours to borrow."

"One book will do," Carol's mom said.

Mr. Linden said that he would make tea and started down the stairs, and her mom went with him.

Carol began to read the titles on the spines of the books. Many seemed interesting. She looked again at the window seat where the book Mr. Linden was reading was lying. Like the others, it was old, its marbled binding fitting perfectly with the dark colors of the room. She picked up the book and read its title: *Tales from a Dark Sea.* There was no author listed. She opened the book where Mr. Linden had placed the flat bookmark. It was page 201 and contained one short paragraph, which, out of curiosity about Mr. Linden, she read.

> *When Esteban grew tired, when his weak leg was harder and harder to kick in the choppy waters, the dolphin would swim ahead of him, slightly to his left, and almost draw him along. He realized how far he was from the shore and how far away the small island in the mouth of the bay still seemed. And yet Esteban had never managed to swim so far before, and the accomplishment filled him with pride and made him try even harder. He wondered if the dolphin knew how proud he was.*

A sentimental story, she thought, one that an older person would find enjoyable. The thought came to her that Mr. Linden must indeed be lonely and that's why he spent his evenings reading. She placed the book carefully down where it had lain before and quickly picked another from the shelf to borrow. When she brought it downstairs, Mr. Linden took it in his hands carefully, almost lovingly, and read the title.

"*Dahomey and the Dahomians?*" he asked, turning the book over in his hands.

"A surprising choice, but that is the pleasure of reading, isn't it? Books have the ability to take the mind to strange places and in strange ways. Well, enjoy it, young lady."

That evening, over dinner, Carol mentioned that she had expected Mr. Linden's library to be stranger.

"You mean with little ivory carvings of mermaids?" her mom asked, smiling.

"I don't know, just the way he goes on about books. He kind of glows when he talks about them. And did you see the way he handled the book I borrowed?"

"Book lovers love books!" her mother announced. "There's a romance about the books—even having them seems to have a kind of excitement."

The book on Dahomey, especially the story about the little African girl brought to England, had been quite interesting, and Carol was eager not only to find another interesting story but also to see what other kinds of books Mr. Linden liked.

It took four calls to Mr. Linden before they found him in.

"He seemed pleased that you liked the book," Carol's mother said. "He asked if we would prefer tea or coffee. I insisted that we didn't need either, of course."

"Oh, I wouldn't mind discussing books over a cup of tea," Carol said. "It fits my image."

"Today's image," her mother teased. "Tomorrow we'll go see Mr. Linden, you'll make a selection, and we'll be out of his hair. Agreed?"

Carol agreed.

During the night she wondered if Mr. Linden missed going to sea, and by the time she and her mother started off for his place she was convinced that he did miss the adventures of his youth.

The rain had pushed the tide up the shore somewhat and had left a residue of tiny, crablike creatures and kelp along its edges, as well as the familiar scent of the sea, which Carol had always liked. As they approached the house her mother nudged her, telling her to look toward the library window. There was Mr. Linden, his dark frame nearly doubled, sitting in the window seat, completely absorbed in his reading.

"The Dahomians seem a bit strange," Carol told him after he invited them in. "But colorful."

"It was the author's opinion of them," Mr. Linden said. "I've met a lot of them in my travels, and they're not very strange these days."

Mr. Linden gestured toward the stairs that led to his library and went to the fireplace, where he began to straighten the logs with a poker. Carol went up the stairs, past the ancient yellowed wallpaper and the corner table, where a pipe smoldered in an onyx ashtray.

She opened several books to see if they contained pictures and found one, *A Narrative of the Cruise of the Yacht Maria Among the Faroe Islands.* The book looked interesting, although at first glance she could see that there were a number of words she would have to look up. She was about to start downstairs when she noted the same book from her previous visit on the seat in the window where Mr. Linden had left it.

Carol picked up the book and opened it to the bookmark. It was still on page 201, but the text now ended farther down the page than she had remembered.

For a while Esteban's mind had wandered as the dolphin circled about him, sometimes lifting its sleek body from the water so that it was merely a dark silhouette against the distant sky. The rhythm of the sea, of the waves brushing across his body, had lulled him into a pattern that made time seem to slow to the easy pace of the tide. When Esteban stopped and lifted his head, he saw for the first time that there were trees growing on the island. But when he turned back toward the shore a sense of panic filled his chest and his heart began to beat quickly. Could he make it back? The dolphin swam around him, the late-afternoon sun sparkling on the water dripping from its body. Its mouth wide open, it appeared to be smiling. Esteban was worried, and his leg began to ache again as he turned for the shore.

Startled, Carol turned over the book and studied it from as many angles as she could. It looked the same as the book she had handled before, but the ending of the story had changed.

Taking a deep breath, she calmed down. There had to be a logical explanation. It was as if she had remembered a previous day but had mixed that day with another.

"I'm glad to discover another reader," Mr. Linden said downstairs in the kitchen. He cradled a cup of tea in his hands. "We are a dying breed, I'm afraid."

That night Carol's sleep was disturbed by troubled dreams. Carol dreamt of sitting in Mr. Linden's library, questioning him about his life and all the books in his library. Then she awoke and lay in the darkness of her room, thinking of the book on the window seat and how she must have allowed her imagination or some random thought change the way she remembered the page.

All things made sense. There were no mysteries in the real world. She thought of mentioning the book to her mother but decided against it. It was her mystery, and she rather enjoyed the curiousness of it all.

The next time they were supposed to visit Mr. Linden, Carol's mother wasn't feeling well. She had one of the headaches that plagued her when the weather grew heavier, just before the late fall and temperatures plummeted the town into its annual winter doldrums. Now that her mother knew more about Mr. Linden, she was fine to let Carol go by herself.

As she made her first trip alone to Mr. Linden's house, turning aside from the wind that rippled the bay, Carol thought about asking him directly about the book. Perhaps she would start by talking about the last book she had borrowed. But not at first, of course. First she had to get her hands on his book and check it out.

She hoped he would allow her to go into the library alone, and he did. She held her breath and walked more softly, almost sneaking up on the books that awaited her.

She glanced at the window seat. The book was still there, angled so that the sun cast a shadow diagonally across the title. She turned away from it, allowing her glance to capture it now and again as she read the titles of the shelved books.

She found a book with small drawings of ships and islands, *The Traveler's Guide to Madeira and the West Indies,* and leafed casually through it, all the time listening for sounds from below. When she heard the clinking of the metal teakettle against the stove, she moved quickly to Mr. Linden's book.

Esteban told himself that he had been swimming long enough. He had already gone much farther than anyone he knew, even farther than men with strong legs. No one swam all the way to the island. Now he was nearer than he had ever been, but it no longer seemed important to him. It was as if he were swimming not for himself but for the dolphin that went before him most of the time but sometimes behind him, nudging him forward.

He began breathing hard, showing the dolphin how tired he was, how afraid he was to keep going when he wasn't at all sure of himself. He was not that strong and had already done more than he had ever done in his life. He stopped and treaded water for a while, with the dolphin only a few feet away. Esteban felt that he and the dolphin were on a mission together, that they were proving something. But what were they proving, and where would it lead?

Again Carol checked the number on the page, even looking at the numbers of the pages before and after the one she was reading. She was right; the story had changed. It was changing from day to day! The boy in the story was swimming out farther each time, and the dolphin swam with him, as if it knew something special about the boy's mission. But how could the story be different each time she read it?

She grabbed the book she would borrow, holding it with both hands, and carried it down to Mr. Linden.

"Ah, George Miller's travel adventure from the age of sail." Mr. Linden examined the book over the rimless glasses he wore. "Excellent choice."

"What are you reading?" Carol asked. "Something about dolphins, I think."

The old black man looked quickly away. For a long moment the room was engulfed in silence. In the distance, barely audible, the gentle lapping of the low tide on the graveled shore came rhythmically.

"It's not a very good book." His voice was lower than it had been. "You wouldn't be interested."

"I am," she said, resolutely. "I am interested."

"Yes, I hear it in your voice, child. I hear it clearly. But let me tell you —warn you, even—that there are books like frigates, that carry the mind gloriously across oceans of ideas," he said. "And then there are books—a few books, I would say—that capture more of the mind than one would want to surrender, books that are better off never read, never opened."

"That doesn't make sense!" Carol said.

"Sense? No, I suppose it doesn't," Mr. Linden said. "But it doesn't make sense to reach my age and discover that everything doesn't make sense, either.

"You can keep that book you're holding," he went on. "It's a fun book. He made drawings of the ships he encountered and the places he visited. Words and pictures. You can't ask for more than that, can you?"

Carol felt as if she were being dismissed and was angry with herself for not being more careful with Mr. Linden. She thought of not taking the book she held, but finally managed a smile, put on her jacket, and started home.

Josiah Linden died on a bitterly cold winter's day. His funeral was held at the Baptist Church on York Street, and more people came than anyone imagined could have possibly known him. Many were sailors and others were just townspeople who remembered him from the time when the town was busier.

The house was sold, and the proceeds, according to the old man's will, went to a charity for aged seamen. A dealer from Westport made an offer for the books. Carol told the dealer that she had been a friend of Josiah Linden's.

"I would love to buy one of his books as a keepsake," she said.

"Well, you're welcome to take any one book you'd like," he replied. "I always like to encourage young people to read."

She searched for the book, checking every title and even behind the rows of books that still stood, waiting as if they expected Mr. Linden to return and reach a dark hand to take one of them down from the shelves. When she didn't find the book, she was very disappointed and for a brief moment thought of taking another book just as a keepsake, as she had suggested.

But then she thought about the book and her fascination with it. She had heard that he had died in bed, and she went into the small room in which he had slept. She looked around quickly and spotted a corner of the book sticking out from under the pillow.

"It's about dolphins," she said to the man that now owned Mr. Linden's library.

The man glanced at the book and nodded approvingly.

"You should try *National Geographic*," he said. "I think I remember a series on dolphins."

Carol smiled.

At home she put the book under her own pillow and waited until that night before turning to the page 201, the bookmark still in place.

The late-evening sun, spreading across the bay and behind the island, lay before him. Esteban had already turned and saw that the shore he had left, his shoes and the sandwich he had brought to the water's edge, were too far away for him to reach. The dolphin sensed it as well, and the two of them swam, Esteban with some difficulty as his arms tired, the dolphin with ease, through the dark waters, toward whatever was on the island. Esteban had heard stories about treasures being buried there, about exotic birds, wildflowers, and even the graves of hermits who had lived there. He didn't know for sure, but he did know that he would reach the island after so many times trying. And even if no one believed him, he would know that the dolphin would have seen him and that maybe, just maybe, all the dolphins in the ocean would know as well.

In the morning, if all went well, he would try to return to the shore from which he started.

In the waning light he could still see the shadow of the dolphin as it swam ahead. Would it be there in the morning to help him back?

Carol put the book down and closed her eyes. Then she opened them again and began to read slowly. The story went on about how the boy awoke in the morning, cold and alone and hungry, and how he had seen not one but two dolphins in the bay, but neither was very close to where he stood on the island's edge. Carol wanted Esteban to be safe, and to make it back to the shore. She wanted the dolphins to help him, but she wasn't at all sure they would.

Mysteries were about finding out how they ended, not new and more difficult mysteries that kept going on and on. She looked at the book and then threw it down on her bed, telling herself that she would never pick it up again. Now she knew why Mr. Linden read the same book every day. He had warned her about the book. Now it was too late.

She lay quietly in the darkness of her room. Now and again her hand would reach out from under the covers toward the light by the side of her bed.

"Don't open the book again," she pleaded with herself. "Please."

From the far side of the bay, the town had grown dark. Occasionally a truck made its way along the winding road or the reflection from the lighthouse through the fog could be seen. Other than that, all was dark, the occasional flicker of a small bedroom light hardly noticeable.

HB

The Seven Chairs

The fifth one ended up in France.

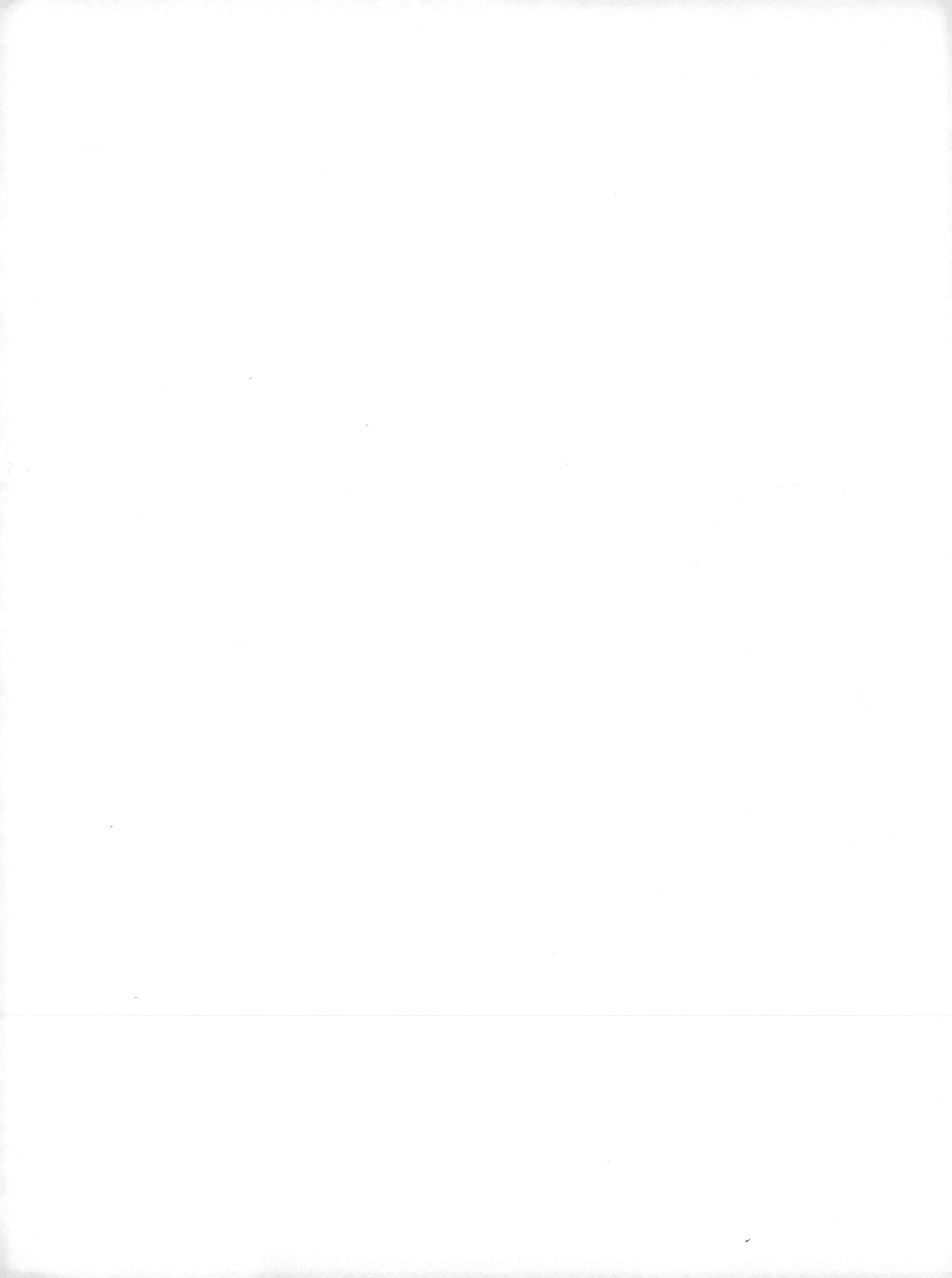

THE SEVEN CHAIRS

LOIS LOWRY

It occurred for the first time in 1928, in a hospital in Wilkes-Barre, Pennsylvania. No one noticed except a sleepy maintenance man shoving a push broom down the hall, past the nursery, at three a.m. He was startled by it and drew a quick breath. But since he had fallen slightly behind in his work and still had the whole OB/GYN floor to do before he could take a cigarette break, he looked away. He nudged a gum wrapper loose from the leg of a chair by the hall window with his broom bristles, and continued methodically on without saying a word. Within the hour he had forgotten it entirely.

Two days later, a nurse named Jean Vargas in Tampa noticed it.

"Did you see that?" Her hands were full—she was preparing bottles for the newborns—and she gestured toward a bassinet with her head.

"What? You mean Gonzales? I just changed her. She's asleep." Victoria Patterson, RN, glanced down at dark-haired Baby Girl Gonzales, who lay on her back with one chubby hand nestled beneath her chin. Her eyes were closed.

"Is she okay? You sure?"

Victoria nodded and picked up a newborn labeled Baby Boy O'Brien. She headed for the changing area. "She's fine. Why?"

"I thought she..." Nurse Vargas hesitated. She didn't know how to describe what she had thought. Maybe she had imagined it. *Surely* she had imagined it. Maybe she had a migraine coming on; sometimes those caused visual distortions—a shimmering in her peripheral vision. She would take an aspirin, she decided, first chance she had.

"No. Never mind. It was nothing." She turned back to what she was doing and chuckled slightly at her own imagination. For a moment she had thought she had seen, out of the corner of her eye, Baby Girl Gonzales float upward and hover in the air briefly before descending again into the bassinet.

Actually, she had seen exactly that. It happened everywhere, that year, but was so fleeting, so momentary, that it went unnoticed by sleep-deprived parents. It was baby girls, always. Little Betsy or Caroline would, without warning, ascend briefly from the padded floor of a playpen, then blink in surprise, giggling, as she plopped back down beside her stuffed bunny. High chairs presented a problem, and sometimes Judy or Peggy, chin smeared with oatmeal, would whimper as she attempted liftoff but was thwarted by her own dimpled knees against the underside of the tray.

Gradually, though, as toddlers, they forgot. Their attention turned to walking, talking, allergies, tantrums, and potty training. Perhaps in their dreams they remembered and re-experienced the wonder and exhilaration of hovering above their own sedentary, diapered lives. But they were earthbound now. There was so much else to do, to learn. The astonishing moments of brief soaring became fragile memories buried deeper and deeper until, like recollections of birth itself, they were too deeply hidden to call back.

Except for Mary Katherine Maguire.

Mary Katherine was a piece of work. That's what her exasperated mother, a housewife in Lowell, Massachusetts, always said about her third child. The first two Maguire children were fun-loving, freckled-faced sons named Michael and James. They were baseball card collectors, altar boys, and Cub Scouts. They had dirty fingernails and skinned knees most of the time. Their mother loved the boys but she had yearned for—had *prayed* for—a little girl with curls and a sweet disposition. What she got, instead, was Mary Katherine.

MK, as she came to be known, did not take no for an answer. Before she could talk, she pouted and stamped her feet if things didn't go her way. Later, with an increasing vocabulary, she argued. Incessantly. She argued with her brothers, who ignored her; with her mother, who tried to reason with her; with her father, who punished her; and with her teachers, the Sisters of Notre Dame. The sisters hid their feelings (they actually admired Mary Katherine greatly—"She has a spirit to her, doesn't she?" one said at dinner one evening) behind stern faces and tried to direct the child's fervor and passion toward good works.

None of them noticed that MK had an astounding talent. It was the same one that all infant girls had once had and had forgotten. Only MK remembered. She practiced. Alone in her bedroom, supposedly doing her homework (she complained that her brothers were a distraction; she needed to be by herself), she would will herself airborne. It was easy for her now, after so much rehearsal. She could lift off and within seconds be gazing down at her spelling book.

Always adventurous, she tried variations. She tried closing her eyes and hovering blind. (It took a moment to get her balance, but she could do it, though she decided it was dull. The fun was in looking down.) She tried circling but found that returning to her chair was difficult if she ended up facing the wrong direction. She needed, MK decided, to work on her form. She had a distinct feeling—a sureness—that she could propel herself to greater altitudes and greater distances. To the ceiling, watching out for a head bump, of course. Over to the corner of the room, above her bed. To the window. *Through* the window! All of that was possible, MK felt. But for now she would concentrate on perfecting her liftoff, making it smooth and silent, keeping a level altitude (tilting was awkward, and made her a little dizzy), and landing back in the chair neatly and without mussing her clothes.

Mary Katherine did not feel guilty or secretive about her peculiar skill. It was not like her brother Michael's nose-picking habit, which he had taken to doing furtively to avoid his mother's outraged slap. It was not like her father, who now and then announced that he needed to check the mileage (or tires, or battery) on the car and disappeared into the garage, where they all knew he was smoking a forbidden cigarette.

It was, for MK, more like a pleasurable, solitary hobby. Like elderly Mrs. Kuzminski next door, who played the piano in the afternoons. Everyone could hear her, especially in summer when the windows were open, and she played pretty well. But if you happened to be there, maybe visiting in her kitchen, and asked her to play something, she said no. It was something she preferred to do alone.

Or the way MK's Aunt Eunice played solitaire. She never played when anyone else was there, though she left the cards on the table if you visited, and you knew that the instant you left she would move the red jack onto the black queen.

Sometimes, though, at her desk, at school, it amused MK to ascend slightly. Not far enough for anyone to notice. Maybe an inch or two. Once, on a hot spring day, she had pulled the skirt of her St. Pius uniform loose and fanned herself with it when Sister was looking the other way. Then she lifted off just a tiny bit, during arithmetic.

And once, just for a private laugh, she had done it during confession. There, in the tiny closed space, murmuring to Father O'Connor about how she had sassed her mother on Thursday, stolen a quarter from her brother James on Friday, and argued with Sister Annunciata on Monday and Tuesday—well, actually *every* day, Father—MK had willed herself upward. First an inch, then another and another, until she was quite high, and if he had peered through the grill (she peered, herself, and could see that he wasn't even looking in her direction) Father O'Connor would have been surprised to see that his eyes were suddenly level with MK's *hips* instead of the top of her unruly brown hair! She let herself down in time to hear her penance and his suggestion that she be kinder to Sister Annunciata, who was getting old and nervous and needed special consideration.

She had always thought of it, this special skill she had, as *rising*. At age two, in her crib, barely verbal, she had said to herself, "Rise!" as she lifted her pajamaed self into the air for a gleeful moment. Now, in fifth grade, she knew that she didn't need to say the command, but it helped, somehow, to describe it to herself. "Rising now," she would whisper toward her desk, as if apologizing to her spelling book that she would be briefly unavailable.

When MK was twelve, in seventh grade, she discovered that in some cases she did not need, actually, to separate herself from the chair. She could, astonishingly, will the chair itself to rise *with* her. This was more comfortable than a chairless rise, and less frightening. Sometimes, chairless, she felt slightly dizzy and faint, looking down; but with a firm chair seat beneath her, she was more secure at great heights. This was important because by now she was occasionally, at night when no one could see, leaving her bedroom through the open window, and sometimes found herself rising to startling altitudes from which she could look down at rooftops.

This was not true, however, of every chair. Most were firmly rooted and stayed so while MK hovered over them. The blue upholstered chair in the Maguire living room never budged, though often, when she was alone at home, MK rose from it and examined the ceiling light fixture from above (there was a dead moth inside the square frosted glass below the bulb). The blue chair simply didn't move.

She tested chairs everywhere for years and determined, eventually, that there were only seven chairs—no more—that could rise.

One was the wooden desk chair in her bedroom; she could ride it up, through the window (she and the chair had to turn and go horizontally, leaving the house) and into the night. It became her most-used rising chair.

A metal folding chair in the church basement had the power, but she disliked it. It looked exactly like ninety-nine other folding chairs and was hard to find, especially when they were stored.

The third was in the basement of the Maguire house. It was a dusty dining room chair with a broken leg that her father had always intended to fix. MK could rise easily with it despite the broken leg, but the basement was boring and smelled moldy, and she was nervous about spiders.

The fourth chair was at her school, in the music room. She tested it secretly once when she was early for band practice and the room was empty. The chair rose without hesitation. But the school was a dangerous location: too many people everywhere, and Sister Charlotte, the principal, was ill tempered. MK had had several encounters with Sister Charlotte and didn't want to press her luck, so she put the music room chair out of her mind.

Chair five she happened on by pure chance. (Or was it? She would wonder for years.) MK's Great-Aunt Helen was visiting from Cleveland, and her parents were desperate to entertain the elderly woman during her three days with them. They took her all the way to Boston one evening to the symphony, which she enjoyed, and one afternoon the whole family watched Michael and James play soccer, but it was clear that Aunt Helen was bored by that. Finally, on the last day of her visit, a Saturday, Mrs. Maguire suggested a trip to the antique store on Pawtucket Street. MK went along.

Great-Aunt Helen was a lover of antiques. She examined every china teacup, each picture frame, soap dish, lace tablecloth, and old photograph in the shop. MK became bored. She wandered off through a curtained doorway into a larger room in back. This was actually an old attached barn, where horsehair settees and pine armoires stood side by side with desks and chests in the dim light. In a cobwebbed corner she found a small mahogany chair with carved legs and a frayed maroon velvet seat.

MK was looking only for a place to rest and wait. She didn't even think about rising. But the instant she sat down on the somewhat lumpy seat of the chair, she knew she had happened on something special.

Always before, she had initiated the rising—had commanded her little desk chair to leave the ground, had sometimes argued it into the air. But this small chair had its own strong will. It *wanted* to rise. It was as if it had waited for years for Mary Katherine Maguire. She was barely settled when it took off, almost toppling her in its eagerness. Perched on the chair, she explored the rafters of the barn (hornets' nest; squirrel droppings) and skimmed the tops of the tall chests. She stubbed her toe on the brass finial of an eighteenth-century clock as she glided past. Suddenly, hearing voices approaching from the front room of the shop, MK ordered the chair to the floor and it obeyed, returning her to the corner where they had found each other.

Driving back home with her mother and great-aunt, MK counted the blocks to Pawtucket Street, decided that it was a walkable distance, and vowed to visit the fifth chair again as soon as she could.

Chairs six and seven, which she identified a few days later, were unremarkable. They were in the waiting room of the orthodontist's office, fake leather, side by side. Testing them while she waited to have her braces tightened, MK felt their possibilities. They could rise. But there was no place to go—just an acoustic tile ceiling—and nothing to look down on except a stack of *Highlights for Children.*

And that was it. Seven chairs.

Two weeks after her Aunt Helen's visit, at her first opportunity, MK walked the fourteen blocks to Pawtucket Street, only to find that the fifth chair was gone.

The proprietor of the antique store, when she asked him, wrinkled his forehead. "Which one?" he asked. MK pointed to the corner of the barn.

"Oh. Yeah. That one. Guy came in, wanted it shipped. Lemme look." He went to a stack of papers on his desk, rifled through them, and then showed her the invoice.

Paris. The fifth one ended up in France.

Time passed. MK thought less often about rising. There were so many other things to think about during her adolescent years. At fifteen she shrieked and squealed at the sound of Frank Sinatra's voice, along with all of her friends. At sixteen she briefly considered the possibility of running off to marry Anthony LaPaglia, who had graduated from St. Benedict's, joined the U.S. Navy, and was going to the war in the Pacific so she might never see him again and her heart would break. But Anthony didn't answer her letters. Neither did Frank Sinatra. Eventually she put them both out of her mind and reconsidered her future.

The sisters at St. Pius were delighted when MK, at seventeen, confided in them that she felt a calling. A vocation. Ancient Sister Annunciata, with whom she had argued so often, enveloped her in a hug so enthusiastic and prolonged that MK almost suffocated in the thick black cloth of the billowy habit. But she came up for air, entered her postulancy, tried to stop arguing and learn obedience, and eventually took her final vows. She became a teaching sister. Her specialty was French.

By 1962 Sister Mary Katherine (for she had been permitted to keep her baptismal name) was middle-aged. She wore bifocals, and had minor stomach problems from time to time. She avoided rich desserts. Most evenings she busied herself with reading, or correcting papers. Her life was orderly and ordinary, except for one thing.

Occasionally now, alone in her room, she willed herself upward into the air, simply hovering slightly above her bed in her nightgown in order to enjoy the buoyant air beneath her instead of the scratchy, overstarched bed linens.

She knew by now, having read of past saints and sisters such as Teresa of Avila, and seventeenth-century Maria Villani, that what she practiced was called levitation. Sister Mary Katherine didn't much care. *A word is a word is a word,* she told herself with a shrug. In her mind, she still thought of it as "rising."

But now when she rose, she began to feel part of a larger community. Not the Carmelites of Saint Teresa, or Sister Maria Villani's Dominicans. Not her own order, either, or the great body of Christians across the earth. Not the unbaptized of Africa, those poor heathens she was supposed to pray for (and did). Not Democrats or Girl Scouts or the League of Women

Voters. Those were all perfectly good groups, of course, she said to herself primly. But this—what she felt part of—was a collection of people yearning for something, something they had once had, something they had forgotten. It puzzled her.

Then, one morning, quite to her surprise, she was called in by Mother Superior and told that she was to go to France the following week. She was handed a plane ticket with her name on it, and given a passport and instructions. It was not newsworthy, just a brief trip—she would be gone only five days—to attend a meeting of French scholars. Sister Mary Katherine had written, after all, a definitive paper on François de Salignac de la Mothe Fénelon. It had attracted a bit of attention and brought some prestige to her teaching order. And so, dutifully, she packed her bag and went.

On her first day in Paris, still slightly jet-lagged and preparing her thoughts for the next day's conference, Sister Mary Katherine took a walk. She walked with her head lowered slightly, practicing humility; Mother Superior had suggested that she do this, along with biting her tongue if she felt inclined to argue.

Quite unexpectedly, for she was not following a map or a guide, she found herself in front of a Gothic cathedral. The massive wooden doors were open, and she noticed a group of tourists wearing sturdy shoes, with a guide speaking German to them, just leaving. Quietly, she entered the vast, silent space, with its vaulted ceiling. The stone floor was dappled by colored light from stained-glass windows. Surprisingly, there was no one inside. Perhaps, she thought, it was the time when tourists stopped for lunch, or to rest. As for clergy—well, most of the religious leaders in the world seemed to be in Rome at the moment, for an important meeting convened by Pope John XXIII.

(With permission of her Mother Superior, Sister Mary Katherine had submitted a formal request, actually, asking if she might attend the Second Vatican Council. Such an important meeting would surely affect her and her fellow sisters, and their futures. But her letter hadn't even gotten a polite reply. It was met with silence.)

She dipped her fingers in the basin of holy water and made the familiar sign of the cross on her habit, then ventured farther down the center aisle.

At the same time, from an undistinguished door on the other side of the great cathedral, two priests entered. It was their job to close the front doors and adjust the small sign that told tourists to return after two p.m. They started down the lengthy expanse, grumbling to each other about the task: it was a nuisance; there should be a cleaning person available to handle it; we have better things to do than housekeeping chores like this. They were disgruntled because they had not been sent to Rome. It looked as if stupid Brazil was going to win the World Cup. And they had both had a great deal of wine with lunch.

They frowned when they saw Sister Mary Katherine. One priest rolled his eyes, recognizing her habit as that from an American order. *Mon dieu. Ces Américains!* They hurried forward to tell her she must leave.

She didn't argue. She simply ignored them. Her attention had been drawn, quite suddenly, to something in a shadowy corner of a small chapel on her left. The light was very dim in the windowless recess. Brushing past the pair of priests, she moved toward the chapel, waited until her eyes adjusted, and then gave a gasp of recognition.

It was the fifth chair.

Sister Mary Katherine sat down.

"Madame! It is not permitted!" one priest called in an indignant voice.

She rose.

"Stop at once!" shouted the other, furiously. *"Vous arrêtez-vous! Immédiatement!"*

She rose higher. Slowly, silently, she drifted with dignity from the chapel, then swooped into the nave and past the priests, who stood rigid with outrage. She could have tapped their silly little hats off with her foot if it had occurred to her. But her mind, and her spirit, were elsewhere. She continued to ascend. Finally, at a great height, hovering peacefully aloft in the light from the arched windows, she could feel, again, the familiar sense of being part of a great body of humans in all parts of the world.

They were all female. They were remembering. They were beginning to rise and to soar.

HB

The Third-Floor Bedroom

It all began when someone left

the window open.

THE THIRD-FLOOR BEDROOM

KATE DICAMILLO

MARCH 28, 1944

Dear Martin,

I am a prisoner. Did you know that this would happen when you put me on the train to her? She has very fat ankles, Martin. You insist that she is our aunt, but I don't believe that it's possible for me to be related to someone with such fat ankles. And I'm not lying: I am a prisoner! She locks me in this room. She has a key that she keeps in her apron and she uses it to lock the door behind her; and after the door is locked, she rattles the doorknob, checking herself. I can feel the rattling of that doorknob in my teeth. I have extremely sensitive teeth. I don't know if you remember this about me. Sometimes I worry that you won't remember me at all.

In any case, you might like to know that the room (my prison!) is on the third floor. I can see mountains. There is some consolation in that (the seeing of mountains), but not enough that you should think I feel cheerful. I don't. I feel abandoned. In fact, my feelings of abandonment are at this very moment so profoundly overwhelming that I am forced to bring this letter to a close. Mrs. Bullwhyte taught us that all good letters should end with a summation, followed by an offering of good wishes. Here is my summation: I am a prisoner. The "relative" who is keeping me prisoner has fat ankles. Also, I didn't mention it earlier, but I am sick. Here are my good wishes for you: I hope you don't get shot.

Cordially, your sister,

Pearlie George Lamott

P.S. What do they feed you in the army? Who feeds you? I am a good cook. I could have taken care of myself while you were away.
P.P.S. I didn't bat an eye when Ma left, did I? I expected it, Martin. But I did not ever expect that you would leave me.

March 29, 1944

Dear Martin,

Here is a sketch of the wallpaper in my prison. As you can see, there is a bird and then another bird and then another bird and then another bird. There is a vine and then another vine and then another vine and then another vine (although it could all be the same vine; it's impossible to tell for certain and I've given up trying). There is a word for this wallpaper and that word (one of Mrs. Bullwhyte's vocabulary words, which she would be happy to see me make proper use of) is relentless. *The wallpaper is so relentless that when I close my eyes against it, I still see it. Even if I weren't locked in this room, I would feel as if I were imprisoned here due to the relentlessness of the wallpaper. It's as if the whole room is under the spell of some witch (a witch with fat ankles). Do you know that once Mrs. Bullwhyte said about me (in front of the whole class) that she has never known a child with such a propensity for verbiage? It pleased me inordinately when she said that. But I must tell you that since I have arrived here, I have not spoken one word. Not one, Martin. Bringing this letter to a close, I will say, in summation, that I am caught in the lair of a witch. My good wishes to you (the recipient of this letter) are that I continue to hope you don't get shot.*

Your sister,

Pearlie George Lamott

P.S. You should know that I am very sick. This happened when I set out to try to find you. I was outside for one full night and it was very rainy and I slept in the crook of a tree and I caught a cold. (Mrs. Bullwhyte said that it is a superstition, an old wives' tale, that you can catch cold from merely being cold. I am sorry to disappoint her, but that is what happened to me.) I didn't believe when I set out to find you that I would actually find you. But I felt duty-bound to look. I want to be clear. (Mrs. Bullwhyte said that we should always strive for clarity of language, as it is a gift to our reader.) So here I am, being clear, Martin: I wasn't running away. I was running toward.
P.P.S. I wonder if those wallpaper birds feel as trapped as I do. It's hard for me to breathe in here.

March 30, 1944

Dear Martin,

Today the doctor came. Don't ask me his name. I can't remember it; but I think it begins with an F. *All I can tell you for certain is that he is a nose whistler. Various and assorted tunes came out of his nose as he examined me. At one point, he got through most of "Begin the Beguine," although I'm not sure he intended any tune at all. He does not, by nature, seem like the kind of man who likes a song.* Dour *is the Bullwhyte vocabulary word that could be properly used to describe him. He listened for a long time to my lungs, but I don't know how he could have heard anything at all over the whistling of his own nose. In any case, I believe that he is looking in the wrong place, as whatever is wrong with me has nothing at all to do with my lungs. The only good that came of his visit is that he said I must have fresh air, and so the window in my room has been opened. Mrs. Bullwhyte once read us a story that started with the words "It all began when someone left the window open." I can't remember a thing that happened in that story. But I've been singing those words to myself now like a song, "It all began, it all began, it all began when someone left the window open." I have never smelled air so sweet, Martin. If I could, I would fly away. Not toward. Away.*

Your sister,

Pearlie

P.S. Instead of a summation, I'm offering this interesting piece of information. I guess it is best that you hear it from me (as opposed to hearing it from "Aunt" Hazel). I bit the doctor. It surprised everyone. It surprised even me. He provoked me. He accused me of being feral. "Has she been raised by wolves?" he said when I refused to answer his questions. She (the fat-ankled "Aunt" Hazel) tried to defend me. She said that I was, for all intents and purposes, an orphan. The doctor said that that was absolutely no excuse, and that at twelve years of age I was almost grown and should act like an adult and speak when spoken to.

In any case, that is neither here nor there (as Mrs. Bullwhyte said to me often enough when I rambled on attempting to explain something that turned out not to be explainable at all). What matters is that I thought I would live up to the doctor's expectations of me and act as if I were raised by wolves, and so I bit him. It was only a small bite, not really wolflike at all. I didn't even break the skin. Or, I do not think I did.

P.P.S. Here are my good wishes for you: You can, if you want, describe what it is like to be in the army. I will listen to you. I have always listened to you.

The end of March, 1944

Dear Martin,

Today a big crow came and sat on the windowsill and looked right directly at me. He stared at me so long that I believe he was working to memorize my face. I would like to think that he then flew out of here, over the mountains and over the sea and right directly to you, holding the whole time this picture of me in his dark head and that when he landed beside you, you looked into his eyes and saw me; *and that you could see how angry I am and how sick I am and how positively full and brimming-to-burst with words I am. This is what Mrs. Bullwhyte would call one of my "extended flights of fancy." She said that I am terribly prone to them and often told me that I should rein myself in or the world was bound to disappoint me. And guess what, Martin? She was right. The world has disappointed me. You let yourself get drafted; you have gone off to war. I am alone in the world. In summation: The mountains outside my window look purple sometimes, and sometimes they look blue. The mountains are always offered up in poetry and the Bible as something solid and true, but my thought on that is this: how could anyone trust in something so changeable, blue one minute and purple the next? My wishes for you: Last night, the moon was very low in the sky. It gave off a strange light that made the wallpaper birds seem to flap their wings. Take that and turn it into a wish for yourself, Martin.*

Your sister,

Pearlie

P.S. When you walked away from me at the train station, I watched you for as long as I was able, as long as was humanly possible, and you did not look back, not once. That is when my heart broke. What's wrong with me has nothing to do with my lungs. That nose-whistling, F-named doctor doesn't know what he's doing. It's my heart, my heart. My heart.

I'M NOT SURE WHEN IT IS

Martin,

I have pneumonia and a high fever and it is hard for me to write these words. Everything shimmers; nothing holds still. I hope you appreciate my effort to communicate, Martin. It is our duty and our joy to communicate our hearts to each other. Words assist us in this task. *That is what was written at the top of every one of Mrs. Bullwhyte's vocabulary lists. Aunt Hazel sits with me and cries a lot and communicates with me that way. I have taken pity on her and allowed her to move her chair close to my bed. She is right beside me. In between crying, she talks and tells me astonishing things. For one: our mother was always flighty, even when she was a child (I guess this isn't that astonishing). And that if she (Aunt Hazel) had known that we had been left all alone (she never even knew that Pa had died), she would not have allowed it. She would have come for us. I can't imagine someone coming for us. I'd like to think about it more, but I can't. I can't think about anything right now. I'm so hot. The air coming in the window smells like mountains and the black wings of crows. If I could say something to Aunt Hazel, if I could manage to make myself speak, I would say that I'm not mad anymore, only afraid, and I don't want to leave the world.*

Pearlie

April 8, 1944

Dear Martin,

Aunt Hazel and I were together in the third-floor bedroom for an eternity. This, of course, is hyperbole. But hyperbole is sometimes necessary to get at the truth (It seems odd, doesn't it, that we have to lie to tell the truth better?). But that is neither here nor there. What I mean to say is that I was feverish for a long time and that Aunt Hazel stayed with me for the whole of it. That is a fact. It is also a fact that Aunt Hazel begged me to speak. Begged me, Martin. I have never before in my life had anyone beg for me to speak. It was deeply satisfying, particularly because for most of my life, I have been encouraged (vehemently) to keep quiet.

In any case, what happened was that I was in the grips of the fever, and I had a movie running in my head and what I kept seeing were not old, sad images, the kind you would expect your brain to pull up when you are sick and maybe dying; images such as Pa's funeral, how black everything (the coffin and the trees and his hair, all slicked back) was and the way you sat on a chair in the dining room afterward and put your head in your hands like an old man; or an image of the house the way it looked (curtains blowing and the light forlorn) the morning I woke up and knew that Ma was well and truly gone; or the sight of you, walking away at the train station, never once turning back. I saw none of that. What I saw instead the whole time the fever raged was a moving list of Mrs. Bullwhyte's vocabulary words. Every word looked as if it were etched in fire, necessary and demanding. I couldn't help but think that Mrs. Bullwhyte would be pleased about this. At some point, I started to say the words out loud. Aunt Hazel listened to me with her mouth hanging open, as if I were speaking words she had been waiting all her life to hear. I have never been listened to that way. It's an absolute shame that what I said didn't make any sense. I just said the words, read them from the list, and when I finally stopped, I felt freer, lighter, as if I might float away. Aunt Hazel, seeing this, took hold of my hand.

And then, as I was looking straight ahead, staring at nothing but the wall, an amazing thing happened. One of the birds broke free. It unpeeled itself from the wallpaper and flew around the room, bright as light, and then it went out the open window. Another bird lifted its wing off the wall and Aunt Hazel squeezed my hand so hard that it hurt, and after a minute, the bird sighed and sank back into the wall and stayed.

You will say that this was fever and Mrs. Bullwhyte would say that it was an extended flight of fancy, but I can only tell you that it is true: what was nothing but paper transformed itself into something living right before my eyes. I fell asleep then, and when I woke up it was dark in the room and Aunt Hazel was still there by my bed, sleeping, holding on to my hand. Can you imagine that? I've come to believe that her thick ankles are a clue to her character. Stalwart. That is the Bullwhyte vocabulary word for Aunt Hazel. The door to my room was unlocked. I took my hand out of Aunt Hazel's and got out of bed and went to the door and opened it all the way and stepped down the hallway and down the stairs and into the kitchen and made myself a sandwich of cheese and bread. The bread was stale, but I have never in my life tasted such a good piece of cheese. I thought about Aunt Hazel, upstairs, asleep in her chair. She has very large hands, Martin, and she had held on to me so tight. And then I remembered the wallpaper bird, breaking free and flying out the window. My legs got shaky and I had to sit down. I sat there in the kitchen and held my sandwich; and I believed suddenly, fiercely, that I was going to live and so were you. I could feel the promise of this, of our surviving, deep in the enamel of my highly sensitive teeth. I finished the sandwich and went back upstairs and Aunt Hazel was still there, sleeping by my bed, and I said her name again and again until she finally woke up.

Your sister,

Pearlie

P.S. In summation: I am almost entirely well. Aunt Hazel is stalwart. It is April now, at last.

P.P.S. My wishes for you: that when you come home, you will go upstairs with me, to the third-floor bedroom, and let me show you the break in the pattern of the wallpaper, the place where a bird was and should be and is not. This is proof of something, I am sure, although I cannot say exactly what. When you turn away from the wallpaper, I will direct your gaze to the mountains, which are waiting, still, outside my window. As I write these words to you, they are changing again. They are turning themselves green.

Just Desert

She lowered the knife and

it grew even brighter.

JUST DESERT

M. T. ANDERSON

Alex Lee was born on Halloween, and so Halloween was always his favorite day of the year. Other kids groaned every year at the end of August, when the first fall breezes stirred the leaves, when the syrupy heat of summer no longer simmered on the streets. They complained that school was about to begin. When those cool breezes arrived, though, Alex Lee was only excited. It meant autumn was coming, with its chill and its mystery. It meant it was time for changes—a whole new year—and time for disguises and, of course, time for his party and pie. This was until the fall when he turned ten, when everything changed and he lost his appetite for pie completely.

Perhaps what happened was Alex's fault. Perhaps he got his just deserts.

A few days before Halloween, before his birthday, Alex was riding his bike around the neighborhood. He was thinking hard about his costume (alien pirate). In fact, he was thinking so hard about what he'd wear (mutant hands from last year, a bandanna, a goggly-eyed, fanged mask from the Haunt Shack down on Route 7, and a black patch to go over one of his mask's three eyes) that he didn't realize he had gone too far and rolled right out of his neighborhood and that he was lost.

His parents had told him never to go past Lunt Street. He'd forgotten. He stopped and looked around. He was on a wide avenue where the trees turned gold. He was way past Lunt. He was in forbidden territory.

He was just turning around, a little embarrassed, when something occurred to him: This far past Lunt, he was probably pretty near Route 7. Sure, he wasn't supposed to be here, and his parents were pretty strict, but he figured he could ride around and find the highway. Then four or five blocks from there, he'd be at the Haunt Shack. He could get his eye patch, his blaster pistol, and his monstrous head.

In a way, he thought to himself, his parents would be grateful. He'd be saving them trouble. They wouldn't have to take him to the store themselves. He'd arrive home in an hour with his bag of stuff and they wouldn't even have to think about driving down to the Haunt Shack, sitting at all those stoplights and parking at the strip mall.

He looked around from side to side as if someone were spying on him. Of course, no one was. So he turned and kept on going, pedaling away from safe Lunt and away from his house on Maple Street.

It seemed like a good idea at first, because it felt like an adventure. The sky was blue and the leaves were blazing red and gold. Alex loved that just when everything was about to die, it got beautiful. As if in celebration of his birthday, he thought with a smile.

On Halloween, in two days, he'd be ten, and he would have his party. All his friends would come over in their costumes. His mother would bake him his birthday pie: pumpkin, of course, with ten candles. He and his friends and his older brother, Doug, would make a haunted house for the little kids in the neighborhood. It was going to be a blast.

But soon he looked around and saw that he was completely lost. He had no idea where he was.

There were houses still, and trees, but the lawns looked empty somehow, and there were no cars on the road.

He did not like this neighborhood. No one was around. It was as if the world had died, but quietly.

He was worried now. Time was passing. His parents would notice how late he was. There was no good excuse. And his dad had a bad temper. Alex bit his lip. He kept riding along the empty streets. He saw nothing that he knew.

He turned right abruptly, and that was when it happened.

There was nothing but a bright light. Alex tottered and skidded. He came to a stop.

There was no road in front of him. There was only a straight line across the horizon, and brilliant, burning white.

He couldn't tell if the line was close or far away.

He held out his hand toward it. It was like the world had disappeared.

A truck honked and swerved. Alex fell off his bike. He screamed. The truck was almost on top of him.

It slammed on its brakes.

Alex looked up. He was lying on the ground, half on the road, half off. His head was on grass. He blinked.

A UPS truck idled right next to him. The driver stood by his side, dressed in brown shorts. "Are you okay? You okay, kid?"

Alex flexed his hands. Then he leaped to his feet. He ran around the other side of the truck.

There were streets all around him. No dazzling light. He was on the corner of streets called Vain and Blair.

"What's going on?" the UPS guy asked. "Are you okay?"

"Did you see a burst of light? Like, a flash, and it looked like there was nothing left here anymore?" Alex asked.

The UPS man shrugged. "No," he said. "I saw a stupid kid stop in the middle of the street and stare."

"There was..." Alex didn't know how to describe it. Whatever it was, he had seen it.

"Do you need help or something, kid?" the UPS man asked.

"Can you tell me how to get back to Maple Street?"

"Maple Street. Sure. You're a ways from home."

The man put Alex's bike in the truck and took him back across Lunt, over to Maple. He dropped Alex in front of his house. "Stay out of the road, kid," the man in brown said, driving off. "If you don't know where you're going, stop racing to get there." The truck pulled around the corner and was gone.

That night, Alex thought about what he'd seen. He couldn't explain it. Maybe it was a brain problem. It had looked like everything had fallen away and all that was left was light and flat.

He was determined to figure out what had happened. He decided he would go back. He had to see those streets again.

The next day, when his mom said, "Do you want to go down to the Haunt Shack and get the parts for your costume?" Alex said sure, that would be great, and could they go by way of Vain and Blair?

His mother looked at him oddly. "No," she said. "That's an awful way to go. It's completely out of the way."

"I just... Can't we drive past there?"

"Honey," said his mother, "I have to pick up Doug from football and I don't have time to drive around crazily."

They went to the Haunt Shack in the car. They stayed on streets Alex knew. He bought his mask, his patch, his piratical belt, and his blaster pistol. He wasn't excited about it now, though. He wanted to know what had happened and where the light had come from. He wanted to know if there was something weird in his brain—or if there was something weird on Blair and Vain.

His mother dropped him off at home. She was off to pick up Doug. "Oh," she said, "can you run down to Ferguson's farm stand and buy us a pumpkin for your pie?" She gave him ten dollars. "It doesn't need to be huge. I'm mostly using canned. Thanks, hon. Be good. Remember: not past Lunt."

She drove off.

He looked both ways, up and down the street.

Then he went into the garage and got his bicycle.

He was going over to Blair and Vain before he stopped at Ferguson's. He had to see what was there.

He took his backpack. He soared down the road.

The trees flashed past. The clouds were gathering overhead. It was cold. One more day and it would be Halloween.

He came to Lunt Street and shot right past. He followed the wide, golden avenue. He tried to remember where he'd turned.

He was in the neighborhood now where everything looked dead. It was all neat and clean, but there were no people. There were no cars on the road. Just a few in driveways. And the lawns looked so empty... *Why?* he wondered. *Why?*

Then it hit him: They looked empty because no leaves had fallen on them. They were immaculate. The trees had turned—some were red, some were brown—but in the storms of mid-October, nothing had blown down. Not a leaf. The roads were clean. They were not cracked.

Now that he'd noticed, he was afraid.

The empty houses rolled on past, and there were no cars anymore, and each mailbox had exactly the same set of junk ads sticking out at exactly the same angle.

He came to a cross street and looked to see where he was.

He swiveled to look down the right hand turn—and there was the blast of light again. The flat line.

He skidded to a stop and stared.

This time, it did not evaporate. It held. There was a bright, blank plain in front of him and dazzling light. It was like everything had been destroyed. The only feature left was the line where the empty sky met empty ground. Alex looked behind him and saw houses and trees. He turned back to the glowing horizon. He walked toward it.

And then there was a furious honking, and he realized he was in the middle of the street and was almost mowed down by a truck.

It was the UPS truck. It screeched to a halt.

Alex tried to understand everything that was happening. The UPS guy—the same one, somehow—was yelling at him out the window. The guy climbed down from the cab of the truck and kept yelling at Alex, saying, "*You* again? Would you stop standing in the middle of streets? You heard of the verge?" Behind the truck, the dazzle continued—and Alex ran to see the empty vista.

"Hey!" said the UPS driver, grabbing Alex's hand. "What's going on with you?"

"Don't you see it?" Alex insisted. "Look! There's nothing! Just a flat line!"

The UPS driver turned. He walked around his truck.

He stood with his hands on his hips. "Right here?" he said. "Just a flat line?"

Alex went to the man's side.

There was a normal street. It had a gas station on it, and a mini-mart, and place that sold concrete lawn ornaments. There was a vacant lot where someone had set up a vegetable stand. They were just writing down some prices on a chalkboard.

Alex couldn't speak. He didn't know what to say. He knew he'd seen nothing here but light—like a vision of his town's destruction.

"Is this real?" he asked.

The UPS guy studied him, confused. "Yeah, it's real," the man said. He walked out a few feet and jumped up and down. His work boots clomped on the pavement. "Real," he concluded. "What are you talking about, kid?"

Alex walked out into the road gingerly, as if he expected it to disappear. "Is it . . . ?" He didn't even know what to say.

"Hey! Hey, kid!" the UPS man called. "I said *keep out of the road!* What *is* it with you?"

Alex crossed to the fruit and vegetable stand. Cars whizzed around him, honking.

He stood there, staring at the apples. The fruit and vegetable stand was laid out under a green tarp.

The UPS man pulled the truck into the lot. "I'm taking you to your house and talking to your parents," the guy said, climbing down. "You're going to get flattened one of these days."

"Is this real?" Alex whispered again. The woman who ran the stand—a large woman with a slight mustache—looked at him suspiciously.

"Come on," said the UPS guy. "Let's go. I'm talking to your parents."

Alex turned and confronted the man. "Who are you?" he said. "Who are you, really?"

The man squinted. "I'm the delivery guy," he answered.

Alex picked up a pear and put it down again. He went for the apples.

The woman said, "Not the apples. The apples aren't ready yet."

She bustled over to his side.

"Try the cherries," she said. "They're flavorful."

Alex looked down and saw a stack of pumpkins. And it hit him: He'd buy one here. As proof. He knew it wasn't a dream. He knew he'd seen what he'd seen.

He reached down and picked one up. He hefted it. It seemed light.

The woman made a face.

He handed her money.

And then he looked past her at the gas station.

The gas station was empty. Completely empty. Behind it there were a few feet of tall grasses, and then a featureless, white nothing marked only with a flat line. The glow was brilliant. It lit the windows of the empty gas station so Alex could see the whorls where they'd been scrubbed.

Alex was astonished. Wildly, he looked the other direction.

Past the convenience store, it was the same: nothing but light.

He reeled in astonishment. He grabbed the pumpkin and ran for the truck.

"Okay," he called to the UPS guy. "Take me home. Please. Take me back. Take me back."

"All right. What's the problem?"

"Take me home! My bike..."

"We can put it in the back."

"Take me! I'm on Maple Street. Down Wistlake. Past Lunt."

"I know. Past Lunt."

Alex ran to get into the passenger's seat. He clamped on his seat belt. Over the tops of the trees, he could see a great emptiness. He shut his eyes. He put his hands over them. He hunched down, doubled over, tried to block out that terrible, empty light.

He felt the UPS guy get into the truck. He heard the guy start the engine up.

They pulled out.

He felt them driving.

And suddenly, Alex was afraid. He did not think the UPS man was really a UPS man.

"Where are you taking me?" Alex asked.

"To your house," the UPS guy said, irritated. "You really have got to stop eating so much sugar cereal, kid."

In ten minutes, they were there. The UPS guy got out and rang the doorbell. No one was home. He said he was going to drop Alex's parents a note and tell them what had happened. Alex didn't care. He wanted to get away, to be alone. He took his bike out of the back of the brown van and he unlocked the front door with his key and he said goodbye and a sloppy thank you and he went inside.

He slammed the door shut.

The house was quiet and still.

He had the pumpkin in his arms.

He carried it into the kitchen and put it on the counter.

Then he fled upstairs. He sat on his bed and stared at the carpet.

All evening, he avoided the pumpkin. It sat downstairs on the counter.

His mother called up to him, "Hey, honey! Thanks for getting the pumpkin. You're the best. Did you talk to Mrs. Ferguson?"

Alex didn't know what to answer. "Yeah," he said, and then realized that was a mistake.

"What did she have to say?"

Alex just answered, "Nothing."

He could feel the pumpkin accusing him of lying. He didn't want to go in the kitchen when his mom and dad made dinner. When his dad called him, he went reluctantly down the steps. Doug sat in the living room, yelling stuff at the TV. Alex walked silently by the pumpkin and kept on going. The pumpkin sat as if glaring at him.

The family ate dinner together with the pumpkin on the counter beside them.

Alex felt terrible for going where he wasn't supposed to and for lying to his mom. He didn't know what to do, because now that he'd lied, he couldn't tell them the story about the brilliant light at Blair and Vain, or his vision of emptiness and destruction behind the gas station.

He had to keep silent.

After dinner, his mother asked him to clear the table and wash the dishes while she made his birthday pie.

He didn't want to see her stab the pumpkin. It was like the pumpkin was his sidekick in crime.

He wanted to throw the pumpkin out. He didn't want a birthday pie. He wasn't sure he deserved one.

He picked up all the plates and took them to the sink. His mother got out flour and butter and canned pumpkin to mix with the real.

Alex pulled out all the utensils from the stack of plates and ran them under water. His mother was chatting with him about his costume, but he couldn't even listen.

She picked up a knife and headed toward the pumpkin.

Alex watched miserably as she went to cut the top off.

Then a strange, awful thing happened: As she touched the pumpkin, holding it steady with one hand, it began to glow softly.

She lifted her hand away, looking at the pumpkin with concern. The glow lit her apron orange. She lowered the knife and it grew even brighter.

She looked, mystified, at the pumpkin.

She said to Alex, "You didn't get this at Ferguson's, did you?"

Alex didn't answer.

"Look at this," said his mother. She touched it and the radiance grew brighter. She knocked the pumpkin with the palm of her hand. It rocked and spun on its side.

"It weighs almost nothing," she said.

She put down the knife and called for Alex's father. "Ken! Ken, come down and see this!"

Alex's father tromped down the steps while Doug ran in from the living room, saying, "What's up? Is Alex in trouble?"

Both Alex's father and his brother stopped, gobsmacked, and stared at the glowing pumpkin.

While they stared at it, Alex's mother reached out and grabbed at the plump side of the gourd.

Her hand smashed through it. It was nothing but a skin, an image, as thin as foil, and inside it there was nothing but emptiness and light. The light flashed and was gone.

Then the pumpkin skin lay like a burst balloon on the counter, fading to black.

Alex's mother put down the knife and put her hands on her head. She turned to Alex's dad. "What are we going to do?" she asked.

Doug let out a long breath, as if something was really, really wrong.

Alex and his family stood in the kitchen. Alex had no idea what had happened. He had no idea what to do. He knew he was going to have to tell the truth now, but he didn't know how anyone would react. They had all seen it—he was sure of that. They had seen the same light, the same emptiness, that he had seen. He looked from one face to another.

They just looked shocked.

"I didn't..." he said, but didn't get any further.

"You went past Lunt Street, didn't you?" his father accused, raising his voice. "You didn't listen to us, and you went past Lunt!"

"Ken," Alex's mom said, soothingly. "Ken, he's confused."

"We were *trying* to protect you," said his father. "Nothing is *done* over there. Nothing's *finished.* We don't *need* that side of *town.* And you went *over* there, and they didn't have *time* to throw anything *together! What have you done? Huh? What have you done, Alex? Now everything's ruined!"*

Alex backed away from his father. He didn't know what his dad was talking about. He was scared. He felt like he had felt on the edge of all that blank, brilliant space, none of it known.

He turned to his mother. He said, "Mom? What's... what's going on?"

She laid her hand on his father's arm and stepped forward. "Honey," she said, "there's not really any way to apologize for this, but things aren't really like they seem. We haven't been entirely, um, honest with you."

"Oh, man," said Doug. "Here it comes."

"Alex, I want you to listen to me. You probably saw something today. I don't know what. Let's just keep it between the four of us that you know. No one else needs to hear about this. They'd be mad."

Alex whispered, "Who? Who are you talking about, Mom?"

"That's not important," she said gently. "What's important is that you're okay."

Alex said, "Who'd be mad?"

His mother sighed. "You've got to understand, Alex. They're working very hard all the time to make all this stuff for you. Everywhere you go, everything you see, they have to build. I mean, they're real quick about it, but it's a lot of effort. And they'd be really, really angry if they knew you saw through it. It would be like... like finding your birthday presents early, when they're hidden in the closet. Not a good idea."

Alex was agape. "What... what are you... saying?" he asked his mother.

And she explained softly, "You're the only person there is. I mean, the only *real* human being. All of this is set up just to... well... How would you put it, Ken?"

"I wouldn't put it at all," his dad said in irritation. "We shouldn't be talking about this."

"Everything," said Alex's mom. "This town, the next town over, New York City, Montreal—it's set up only for you. There's nothing, otherwise. There's nothing on the other side of the world. No Australia. No France. There's no globe. Nothing but light and a flat plain. Just desert."

Alex reeled. He thought of the emptiness he had seen behind the mini-mart.

Doug asked, "If he knows anyway that there's no France, do I have to keep taking French?"

"Yes, Doug," said Alex's father.

"Alex, honey," said his mother. "How do you feel? How are you feeling?"

Doug kept complaining. "There are like ten thousand ways just to say the word 'it' in French. It's the dumbest language!"

"Doug!" said their father in a warning growl.

"In reality," Doug explained to Alex, "the French people you've met all talk with a kind of Texas accent when you're not around. Then when they see you coming, they just go, 'Flaw flaw flaw fwaah fwaah.' "

"Douglas," said their father, "I am only asking you once more."

Alex didn't know where to run. He didn't know who to talk to. He couldn't talk to any of his friends. He didn't even know who they really were. He couldn't talk to any of his friends' parents. He couldn't go to the police. And if he ran too far—to his grandparents, say—he didn't even know if the world would exist. It might just be a flat line and burning light.

His mom said, "Wherever you went today, you must have forced them to come up with a landscape really quick. They couldn't think things through. They didn't have time to give anything an inside. The pumpkin wasn't really a pumpkin yet." She picked up the dead skin with a finger and put it down again. "The more we concentrated on it, the flimsier it got. Until, *poof!*" She leaned down and pulled Alex to her. "Hey, honey. Honey. I know this is surprising."

He finally asked the question he was most afraid of. "What... what *are* you?" he asked his mother, the person, he thought, who loved him most on earth.

His mother and father looked at each other. He saw that there were tears in his father's eyes. His mother answered gently, "What we are doesn't matter. It wouldn't make sense to you. All that you need to know is that we love you. We really do. We love you so much. As much as you've always thought."

"Even more," said his father. "Alex, we've built the world for you."

Doug muttered, "Even some countries that don't *need* to exist."

"We are not deleting France, Doug," Mrs. Lee said. "That's final." She pulled Alex close. She put her arms around him. He could smell her shampoo. It smelled like it always did, but he didn't even know what she was. He didn't even know what species. He didn't know what her hair was. He didn't know what she knew. He didn't know when she was watching him, or why, or for what. She said, "I know this is confusing, but one thing shouldn't be confusing at all: We really do love you. That's why you're here."

"We may have to..." Alex's father coughed and continued. "We may have to wipe out a day or so of your memory. We'll see how stuff goes. But don't worry. They'll just arrange for you to have a concussion. You know. You'll fall off something."

"It happened before," said Doug. "When you thought you were having a hernia operation. Really, you found out what was going on and you saw one of us like we really are, so we had to make you forget stuff."

"Let's not talk about that," said Alex's mother, and she kept stroking her son's brow, whispering, "We love you, Alex. We love you. We love you more than you can imagine."

So he lay in bed that night, the night before his tenth birthday, staring at the ceiling. He heard his parents downstairs, playing at being parents in case he should hear. In the next room, his brother studied a language that was not spoken anyway in a country that didn't exist.

The next day, Alex would have a party. His friends would all be there. They'd be dressed up in their costumes. Behind their masks would be their faces. But he didn't know what eyes would be hidden behind their faces. He would have to play along. They would be watching.

There was nowhere he could run. They had made every place for him.

He lay in bed, and the minutes clicked toward the moment he would finally turn ten.

You are done with this story now. You can shut the book and make the nightmare go away. That will feel good and secure. You know it is not a real story, of course—because you know that you are not part of a plot to make a whole world for Alex P. Lee of Maple Street, the one human being who exists. You know you have your own thoughts. You know you are real.

So after all, if there were only one actual person in the world, one person for whom the whole illusion is carried on by unknown beings, it would have to be you. And it might be, that if someone wanted to break that news to you gently—someone who thought you should know—they might, of course, slip a story into a book, a kind of message to say, "Watch out." They might contact you this way because no one else will let them speak to you. They might hope you'll read one of the books that are made to ensure that bookshelves and library windows look full to you. A book, for example, of stories by a man who may never have existed, an illustrator who may never have set pencil to paper.

Don't look up in worry. Don't knock the walls to confirm that they are solid. Just turn the page slowly. They're watching.

Don't show them that you know. Please. Don't show them a thing.

Captain Tory

He swung his lantern

three times and slowly the schooner appeared.

CAPTAIN TORY

LOUIS SACHAR

Every morning Captain Tory ate a cinnamon doughnut at the doughnut shop on Church Street, three doors down and across the street from the hardware store. Paul and his mother lived in the apartment above the hardware store, and at 6:17 Paul would look out his window to see Captain Tory leave the doughnut shop and head toward the wharf. "Captain Tory!" he'd shout, and the captain would stop, look around a bit puzzled, and then, seeing Paul in the second-story window, he'd wave. Paul always waved back. He would continue to watch as Captain Tory made his way past the old stone church that gave the street its name and disappear around the corner.

No one had ever seen Captain Tory actually enter the doughnut shop, which didn't open for business until seven. Vanessa LaRouche, the woman who owned the place, would simply turn around and there he'd be, sitting on a stool at the counter. Even after nine years, it still made her heart jump (although she regained her composure more quickly than the first time she saw him). "What can I get you this morning?" she would ask.

"Do you have a cinnamon doughnut?"

"I believe I do."

"And a cup of coffee, if you would be so kind."

"Would you like cream with that?"

"Just a touch."

The fact that he never paid for the doughnut didn't disturb Vanessa. She assumed money was impossible for him, and considered his morning visits a sort of blessing. Indeed, she would be sorry if he failed to appear. Captain Tory had died one hundred and sixty-five years ago when his schooner got lost in the fog and smashed into the rocks below Lookout Point.

Vanessa imagined he had been taking that same walk down Church Street every day for the past one hundred and sixty-five years. His routine must have changed to some degree over the years, however, she reasoned, since the doughnut shop had been in business less than a decade.

Paul's mother owned the hardware store, but she said it was the other way around: "The store owns me." When she wasn't attending to customers, she was managing inventory, ripping apart boxes, updating the window displays, or hauling around fifty-pound bags of cement. She spent most evenings on the computer, desperately trying to balance her accounts. Ten months ago, a giant discount hardware warehouse had opened less than three miles away, and she had to work twice as hard just to keep the store above water. Paul helped out when possible, but besides sweeping the sidewalk in front of the store twice a week, there was only so much a seven-year-old boy could do. She wouldn't let him work the cash register until he turned ten.

Paul's father had died two weeks after Paul's third birthday. Paul's only vivid memory of him was one time, when he was watching his father shave, his father put shaving cream on Paul's face too.

When Paul's father died, Paul's mother, an ex-dancer who had only just recently moved from New York City, found herself to be the unlikely owner of the hardware store. At the time, she didn't know a ratchet from a flange.

But Paul's mother was a "smart cookie." Paul had heard a man call her that, and he would smile whenever the phrase came to mind. His mother learned not only the names of every tool and piece of hardware in the store, but also how they were supposed to be used—*correctly.* Paul felt a sense of pride whenever he listened to her give detailed instructions on how to fix a leaky faucet or patch a section of drywall.

My mother is a smart cookie.

At a quarter past six, Paul, in his flannel dinosaur pajamas, was looking out his window. The sky was still dark, and the streetlights were dulled by a foggy mist.

Because of the overhang, Paul couldn't see the door to the doughnut shop, but he'd be able to spot Captain Tory as soon as he stepped out onto the sidewalk.

He glanced at the clock by his unmade bed just as the time changed from 6:16 to 6:17. He waited. He was still waiting at 6:18. And at 6:19.

Paul felt anxious. This had never happened before. Captain Tory was always on time.

At 6:24, Paul was about to put on his jacket and go to the doughnut shop when at last Captain Tory emerged. Paul had a lump in his throat from all his worrying, and it prevented him from shouting out his usual greeting. As he collected himself, he watched Captain Tory suddenly turn, cross the street, and walk directly toward him. Paul's view became blocked by the blue and white awning that hung above the store, but a moment later he heard what sounded like a knock on the door below.

Paul burst into his mother's bedroom and shook her awake. "You have a customer!"

"What?"

"Downstairs," Paul said. "At the store."

"What time is it?" she asked groggily as she squinted at her clock. "It's not even six thirty!" She pulled the covers over her head.

"It's Captain Tory!" said Paul.

His mother peeked out from under the covers. "Captain Tory, here?"

"Hurry!"

Paul's mother stumbled into the bathroom, where she splashed some cold water on her face. She was still putting on her bathrobe as Paul dragged her out to the utility room behind the kitchen. "I didn't even brush my teeth," she complained.

A narrow stairway led from the utility room to the back room of the hardware store. Three steps from the bottom, Paul's mother pulled on the chain for the overhead light bulb, and then she and Paul made their way around a row of filing cabinets and several stacks of boxes. Paul switched on the main store lights.

They could see the silhouette of a man on the other side of the shade covering the glass door at the front of the store. "Make sure it's him," said Paul's mother. "I'm not opening the door for any Tom, Dick, or Harry."

Paul suddenly felt a little scared as he slowly approached the door. His mother was just a few steps behind him. He pulled back the shade just enough to peek out.

Captain Tory stood straight and tall. He wore a thick wool coat and heavy boots. His neatly trimmed beard and mustache gave his face a distinguished quality, despite its ruddy color and the two-inch scar beneath his right eye.

"It's him," said Paul.

His mother adjusted her robe, then pushed back a few wisps of hair from her face. "Open it," she said, speaking barely louder than a whisper.

The bell jingled above him as Paul opened the door.

Captain Tory removed his cap and held it against his chest. An unlit lantern was in his other hand.

"Good morning," he greeted them.

"Good morning," said Paul's mother.

Paul stood next to his mother, and without being aware of it, found himself holding her hand.

"I'm very sorry to bother you," said the captain. "I realize your establishment usually doesn't open quite this early in the morning."

"It's fine," said Paul's mother.

"I seem to have run out of kerosene," said Captain Tory.

"Kerosene," repeated Paul's mother.

"For my lamp. I'd be most appreciative."

"I can show him," said Paul, suddenly regaining his courage. "I know where it is."

With Paul leading the way, the threesome made their way through the aisles. "There's quite a bit of fog this morning," the captain said. "I will need a bright light and a keen eye."

The kerosene was too high for Paul to reach. He pointed it out to Captain Tory, who retrieved the can from the shelf. The captain, however, seemed baffled by the plastic safety tab, and Paul's mother had to open it for him.

"Talented as well as lovely," said Captain Tory.

Paul noticed his mother's face turn pink.

Captain Tory poured enough kerosene to fill his lamp, then handed the can back to Paul's mother.

She placed the can on a shelf behind the register. "I'll save it for you, for next time," she said.

"Much obliged," said Captain Tory.

"Are you going to be sailing past Lookout Point?" Paul asked.

"Aye."

"Be careful," warned Paul's mother.

Captain Tory smiled and tipped his cap. The bell jingled as he left the store.

A moment later, Paul and his mother stepped out into the empty street and watched him walk away. As he turned onto Pine, all they could see was his lantern, gently swinging through the fog.

He was back the following morning. "I'm very sorry to bother you. I realize your establishment usually doesn't open quite this early in morning. I seem to have run out of kerosene."

By his third visit, Paul's mother had already brushed her teeth, and she and Paul were dressed and waiting for him.

"I realize your establishment doesn't—"

"You need some kerosene for your lamp," Paul's mother interrupted.

"Well, yes. There's quite a bit of fog this—"

"And you need a keen eye and a bright light to sail around Lookout Point."

"Exactly so," said Captain Tory.

One week later as Captain Tory was leaving the store, Paul slipped quietly into the back room, then on out the door. He raced through the alley and reached the street just as Captain Tory was walking past the old church.

"Captain Tory, wait up!"

The captain stopped and looked back. He waited as Paul hurried up alongside him.

As they approached Pine Street, Paul kept his eyes fixed on Captain Tory, whose form seemed to be mingling with the mist. His beard became blurred. His coat seemed to be enshrouded with fog. Before he could completely fade away, Paul reached out and grabbed the captain's hand.

At first touch, it felt something like a burlap glove filled with feathers, but as Paul held on, the hand seemed to firm up, along with the rest of Captain Tory. When they turned onto Pine Street, he was as tangible as he had been back at the hardware store.

Paul smiled at Captain Tory, who smiled back.

"It must be tough to grow up without a father," the captain said to him.

"Me and my mom do okay," said Paul.

"Can't be easy for her," said the captain. "Running a business and raising a child all by herself."

"She's a smart cookie," said Paul.

"Aye, that she is."

"She's pretty too," said Paul.

"Aye."

The fog was beginning to lift when they reached the harbor. Paul could see the lights from the houses on the other side of the bay. There were a few commercial fishing boats, and some private yachts anchored to the docks, but no schooner.

He wondered what Captain Tory would do.

"If you want, you can come back home with me?" Paul suggested. "We have an extra room. You can help out around the store, and my mom's a great cook."

"That's a mighty tempting offer," said the captain. "But my crew is waiting for me." He swung his lantern three times and slowly the schooner appeared.

Paul watched it silently glide to a stop against a dock. He waited on the jogging path above the harbor as Captain Tory went down to it and climbed aboard. Paul heard him calling out instructions to his crew as the schooner moved lightly across the water, in the direction of Lookout Point, then slowly faded from view.

Change happens, sometimes slowly, sometimes in sudden bursts. The following morning, Captain Tory was back again at the hardware store, but instead of a lantern, he held a bouquet of daisies. Within six months he was living in the extra room and proving to be a great help around the store.

Whenever Vanessa LaRouche heard people in the doughnut shop gossip about Paul's family, she would tell them it was none of their business. And while she was sorry that Captain Tory no longer frequented her establishment, every morning she would put a cinnamon doughnut in a white paper bag and leave it outside the door of the apartment above the hardware store.

HB

Oscar and Alphonse

She knew it was time to send them back.

The caterpillars softly wiggled in her hand,

spelling out "goodbye."

OSCAR AND ALPHONSE

The Farkas Conjecture

CHRIS VAN ALLSBURG

The Farkas Conjecture was named for Joseph Farkas (1892–1945), a brilliant and eccentric theoretical physicist who fled Munich in 1939, narrowly escaping the predations of the Nazis. His fate remained a mystery until 1952, when a Swedish naturalist studying the migratory patterns of elk along the Kalixälven River came upon the collapsed remains of a small cabin.

Beneath the pile of bleached and broken birch logs, the naturalist discovered a brass box that contained the journals of Farkas. In them, the scientist had not only described his years of isolation in the Swedish wilderness, but had also laid out the conjecture that has bedeviled the greatest minds in science for more than half a century.

In the journals' final entry, dated April 18, 1945, Farkas indicates he has found the solution to the problem, but feels, before writing it out, that he must check the fishing lines he has hung through holes he'd cut in the frozen surface of the river.

Records indicate the spring of 1945 was unusually mild in the northern parts of Sweden. It is assumed Farkas unintentionally and for eternity joined the fish in the frigid waters of the Kalixälven.

One might describe the Farkas Conjecture as the Mount Everest of unproven scientific theorems, except that Mount Everest has been scaled countless times and not a soul has come close to standing atop the Farkas Conjecture.

It has certainly not been for want of trying. Armies of mathematicians and physicists have spent the better part of their lives and careers, some might even say their sanity, trying to discover an approach that will lead them to the summit of this great puzzle of all puzzles.

What drives them on is their belief that a solution will lead to unprecedented insights into the nature of the physical world, insights with rewards that can scarcely be imagined. Some have claimed that a complete understanding of the conjecture could allow man to control gravity and even manipulate time.

Among the most passionate and dedicated believers in the hidden power of the Farkas Conjecture was the father of thirteen-year-old Alice Randolph. Dr. Julius Randolph was a world-renowned professor of physics who had turned his obsession, his "Farkas fever," into a family business. He sent each of Alice's three older brothers off to college to earn advanced degrees in math and physics. He then summoned them back to the family home every summer. There, the four of them would spend hours in the professor's blackboard-lined study, opening the door only to receive pots of coffee from Alice's mother and to release the clouds of chalk dust produced by their incessant calculations.

Though Professor Randolph had pushed his daughter to follow in her brothers' footsteps, the child simply did not have "a head for numbers." What really held her interest, as her father put it, was "communing with nature."

This was true. For a child her age, Alice was unusually content to spend prolonged periods alone, sitting in the backyard, leaning against a tree and gazing into the distance, or strolling through the woods behind the old Randolph home.

It was on one of these walks that Alice found herself beside a small stream that ran through the woods near her home. She spotted a bird circling just above a leaf that was being carried along in the stream's current. Precariously balanced on the leaf were two caterpillars. Alice knelt beside the water's edge, scaring away the bird and rescuing the two wet and fuzzy creatures.

She placed them on a sunlit rock. Once they'd dried out, they began to move. Alice watched them closely and saw they positioned themselves to form the letter *t*. "That's strange," Alice thought to herself. Then they wiggled around and formed an *h*. This was followed by an *a* and an *n*, until they had spelled out *"thank you."*

Alice lowered herself close to the caterpillars and whispered, "You're welcome." They lay perfectly still. "Are you all right?" Alice asked. They spelled out, slowly, *"very hungry."*

"Of course you are," Alice answered. She gathered up a handful of choice leaves and placed them on the rock. The caterpillars started chewing eagerly. "I know why you are so hungry," she told them. "It's because soon you're going to have to make yourselves cocoons and turn into butterflies!"

The instant Alice said this she felt silly, because of course if anyone knew about that sort of thing, it would be caterpillars. They stopped eating and answered politely, *"yes true hard to believe,"* they paused for a moment, *"we are not sure we will make it."*

Alice understood. They'd certainly had a close call before she rescued them. "I can take care of you until you are ready," she told them, and rose to her feet. "Will you wait here for me until I come back?" The caterpillars seemed to confer, and then spelled out, *"yes we are grateful."*

Alice ran to her house and found an empty glass jar. She poked holes into its lid, then hurried back to the rock. Her new friends were still there. She filled the jar with leaves, then set it sideways on the rock. "You'll be safe in here," she told them. The first caterpillar wiggled into the jar and Alice said, "I think I'll call you Oscar." As his companion joined him she added, "and you will be Alphonse."

Alice was very excited to show her family the spelling caterpillars. She knew her brothers and father were hard at work, but certainly they would want to meet Oscar and Alphonse.

When she went into the study she could tell they were annoyed by her interruption. "But look!" she said. "Look at what I have." The men gathered around Alice as she opened the jar.

"Why, it's just a couple of caterpillars," one of her brothers said. "Wait, just wait," Alice told them.

Oscar and Alphonse wiggled out of the jar and onto the top of a worktable that was covered with sheets of paper bearing endless equations and calculations. The caterpillars stopped moving, and Alice spoke to them. "Go ahead, spell something. Say hello." She gave them a little nudge with her finger, but they just lay there, lifting their tiny heads toward the chalkboards but otherwise remaining motionless. Alice looked up at her brothers, her father, who had already turned away and resumed his work, chalk stick in hand.

"They can spell—really, they can. I saw them do it outside."

"Well, maybe you should take them back outside then," her oldest brother told her. He picked up the paper the caterpillars were on and slid them back into the jar. "Careful!" Alice told him, taking hold of the jar.

Mrs. Randolph appeared at the study door to inform her family that lunch was ready. As the men filed out, Alice held the jar up to her face. "I'm very disappointed," she said.

She put the jar on the worktable and joined her family. From the mealtime conversation Alice could tell that the morning had not gone well for her brothers and father. What had looked like a promising approach to solving the conjecture earlier in the week had turned out to be just another dead end, another "Farkas Phantom," as her brothers referred to the family's failed attempts.

Mrs. Randolph could sense her sons and husband's frustrations. She suggested they take a break from work for the afternoon. Perhaps a long walk would clear their minds. The professor agreed, reluctantly, and after finishing lunch, the men took their leave. Alice, though invited to accompany them, declined. She wanted very much to get back to Oscar and Alphonse and find out if they would still spell for her.

Back in the study, she opened the jar. Oscar and Alphonse climbed out. "Why didn't you say something when I introduced you?" The caterpillars spelled out *"sorry very shy."* Then they lifted their tiny heads once again and stared at the chalkboard. It was filled with equations and notes. Oscar and Alphonse seemed to sway back and forth as they took it all in. Finally they wiggled around: *"we know."* "Know what?" Alice asked. *"The answer"* was their reply.

Alice looked at the chalkboard and then back at Oscar and Alphonse. "To that?" she asked in disbelief.

The caterpillars began moving. *"Watch carefully,"* they spelled out. Alice picked up a pencil and paper. Slowly, Oscar and Alphonse began forming the same strange mathematical signs and symbols that covered the chalkboard. She dutifully and carefully wrote each one down, filling four full pages.

The caterpillars stopped. "Is that it?" Alice asked. *"Not yet,"* they answered, *"very tired very hungry."* Alice helped them back into the jar, where they immediately began chewing on the leaves. They had eaten most of what she had put in the jar, so Alice took them outside to get more, returning to the rock where they had dried themselves out. She heaped leaves onto it. Oscar and Alphonse contentedly munched away. It looked to Alice as if they were growing larger with every bite.

You wouldn't think writing out signs, symbols, and numbers would make a person tired, but Alice was as exhausted as the caterpillars, and the three of them fell sound asleep. Alice did not awake until she heard a voice calling her name.

The sun was getting low in the sky and Alice looked around for Oscar and Alphonse, and found they had climbed back into their jar and were still asleep. She heard her name called out again, picked up the jar, and headed for home.

When Alice stepped out of the woods into her backyard, she saw two of her brothers, hands raised to their mouths, calling out for her. When they caught sight of their sister, they excitedly ran to her. Words tumbled out of them: "Stroke of genius," "mind blowing," "cosmic insight." They pulled her along into the study, where her other brother and her father had just finished filling the chalkboards with the notes that Alice had taken from Oscar and Alphonse.

Her father turned when Alice entered the room. He held up the notes. There seemed to be tears in his eyes. "Alice, Alice, Alice, why didn't you tell us?" "Tell you what?" she asked. "That you…" Her father paused, at a loss for words. "That you knew, that you were working right along with us, but never said a word?" He held the papers up high. "This is a work of genius."

One of her brothers took Alice by the shoulders and looked straight into her eyes. "This is the approach we have been struggling to find. This takes us closer than we have ever been, than anyone has ever been. How did you figure this out?"

Alice was growing uncomfortable accepting praise for something she did not do. "It wasn't me," she answered, and lifted up the jar holding Oscar and Alphonse. "It was them. They showed me what to write down." The men were silent. They didn't know whether to rejoice because Alice, the baby of the family, was the most brilliant person they'd ever encountered, or to be worried, because she apparently believed she could communicate with caterpillars.

But her father was certain of one thing. As remarkable as Alice's progress and calculations had been, she had stopped just short of proving the conjecture, and there were still some steps to take. He knew those last steps could use up another lifetime.

If the only way to get Alice to keep going was to let her pretend that the caterpillars were solving the problem, that was okay with him. He'd spent his life around eccentric and peculiar scientists; he knew how to handle them. So he gently went to his daughter and asked her if she thought her friends might be willing to finish their work. Alice looked into the jar. The overfed caterpillars were sound asleep.

"They're too tired right now, I think. But we can try tomorrow." Her father nodded, and her brothers, humoring her, agreed and told her that was an excellent idea.

Alice climbed the stairs to her room, carrying Oscar and Alphonse. Later her mother came in, to bring her a tray of food and to tell her how proud her father and brothers were.

Alice awoke early the next morning. She looked into the jar. Oscar and

Alphonse had eaten through all their leaves and were lying peacefully at the bottom of the jar. She thought they might like some fresh air, so she got dressed, went outside, and returned to the rock where they had first met. She unscrewed the jar and let the caterpillars crawl onto her hand. She could see how much larger they had gotten in just the day she'd taken care of them. They were ready, any minute, to start making their cocoons, to become what they were meant to be—butterflies. She knew it was time to send them back. The caterpillars softly wiggled in her hand, spelling out *"goodbye."* She helped them climb onto the bark of a small tree and watched as they slowly inched their way upward and out of sight.

The House on Maple Street

It was a perfect lift-off.

THE HOUSE ON MAPLE STREET

STEPHEN KING

Although she was only five, and the youngest of the Bradbury children, Melissa had very sharp eyes, and it wasn't really surprising that she was the first to discover that something strange had happened to the house on Maple Street while the Bradbury family was summering in England.

She ran and found her older brother Brian and told him something was wrong upstairs, on the third floor. She said she would show him, but not until he swore not to tell *anyone* what she had found. Brian swore, knowing it was their stepfather that Lissa was afraid of; Daddy Lew didn't like it when any of the Bradbury children "got up to foolishness," and he had decided that Melissa was the prime offender in that area.

It would probably turn out to be nothing, anyway, but Brian was delighted to be back home and willing enough to humor his baby sister, at least for a while. He followed her down the third-floor hallway without so much as a murmur of argument, and only pulled her braids.

They had to tiptoe past Lew's study, because Lew was inside, unpacking his notebooks and papers and muttering in an ill-tempered way. Brian's thoughts had actually turned to what might be on TV tonight—he was looking forward to a pig-out on good old American cable after three months of the BBC—when they reached the end of the hall.

What he saw beyond the tip of his little sister's pointing finger drove all thoughts of television from Brian's mind.

"Now swear again!" Lissa whispered. "Never tell *anyone*—Daddy Lew or *anyone*—or hope to die!"

"Hope to die," Brian agreed, still staring, and it *was* a half-hour before he told his big sister, Laurie, who was unpacking in her room.

"Sorry," Brian said, "but I gotta show you something. It's *very* weird."

"Where?" She went on putting clothes in her drawers as if she didn't care, but Brian could tell when Laurie was interested, and she was interested now.

"Upstairs. Third floor. End of the hall past Daddy Lew's study."

Laurie's nose wrinkled the way it always did when Brian or Lissa called him that. She and Trent remembered their real father, and they didn't like his replacement at all.

"I don't want to go up there," Laurie said. "He's been in a pissy mood ever since we got back. Trent says he'll stay that way until school starts and he can settle back into his rut again."

"His door's shut. We can be quiet. And if you're really worried about him coming out, we can take an empty suitcase. If he opens the door, we'll pretend like we're putting it in the closet where we keep them."

"What *is* this amazing thing?" Laurie demanded, putting her fists on her hips.

"I'll show you," Brian said earnestly, "but you have to swear on Mom's name and hope to die if you tell anyone." He paused, thinking for a moment, then added: "You specially can't tell Lissa, because I swore to her."

Laurie's ears were finally all the way up. "Okay, I swear."

They took along *two* empty suitcases, one for each of them, but their precautions proved unnecessary; their stepfather never came out of his study. They could hear him stamping about, muttering, opening drawers, slamming them shut again.

But a moment later, when she looked at the place Lissa had pointed out to Brian and that Brian now pointed out to her, she forgot about Lew completely.

"What *is* it?" she whispered to Brian. "My gosh, what does it *mean?*"

"I dunno," Brian said, "but just remember, you swore on Mom's name, Laurie."

She could have strangled him . . . but a promise *was* a promise, especially one given on the name of your one and only mother, so Laurie held on for more than one full hour before getting Trent and showing him. She made him swear not to tell, too, and as the oldest, he had no one *to* tell.

Trent stood, looking at what the other children had looked at before him. He stood there for a long time.

"What *is* it, Trent?" Laurie finally asked. It never crossed her mind that Trent wouldn't know. Trent knew *everything*. So she watched, almost incredulously, as he slowly shook his head.

"I don't know," he said, peering into the crack. "Some kind of metal, I think. Wish I'd brought a flashlight." He reached into the crack and tapped. Laurie was relieved when Trent pulled his finger back. "Yeah, it's metal."

"Should it be in there?" Laurie asked. "I mean, *was* it? Before?"

"No," Trent said. "I remember when they replastered. That was just after Mom married *him*. There wasn't anything in there then but laths."

"What are they?"

"Narrow boards," he said. "They go between the plaster and the outside wall of the house." Trent reached into the crack in the wall and once again touched the metal. The crack was about four inches long and half an inch across at its widest point. "They put in insulation, too," he said, frowning thoughtfully and then shoving his hand into the back pockets of his faded-wash jeans. "I remember. Pink billowy stuff that looked like cotton candy."

"Where is it, then? I don't see any pink stuff."

"Me either," Trent said. "But they *did* put it in. I remember." His eyes traced the four-inch length of the crack. "That metal in the wall is something new. I wonder how much of it there is, and how far it goes. Is it just up here on the third floor, or..."

"Or what?" Laurie looked at him with big round eyes. She had begun to be a little frightened.

"Or is it all over the house," Trent finished thoughtfully.

After school the next afternoon, Trent called a meeting of all four Bradbury children. It got off to a somewhat bumpy start, with Lissa accusing Brian of breaking what she called "your solemn swear" and Brian accusing Laurie of putting their mother's soul in dire jeopardy by telling Trent.

"Hush, all of you," Trent said. "What's done is done, and I happen to think it all worked out for the best."

"You do?" Brian asked.

"Something this weird needs to be investigated, and if we waste a lot of time arguing over who was right or wrong to break the promise, we'll never get it done."

Trent glanced pointedly up at the clock on the wall of his room, where they had gathered. It was twenty after three. He really didn't have to say any more. Their mother had been up this morning to get Lew his breakfast, but afterward she had gone back to bed, and there she had remained. She suffered from dreadful migraines.

She wouldn't see them on the third floor, but "Daddy Lew" was a different kettle of fish altogether. With his study just down the hall from the strange crack, they could conduct their investigations only while he was away, and that was what Trent's glance at the clock had meant.

Lew had left shortly after noon, with a briefcase crammed full of papers, but he might be back at any time between now and five. Still, they had *some* time, and Trent was determined they weren't going to spend it squabbling about who swore what to whom.

Laurie spoke for all of them when she said: "Just tell us what to do, Trent—we'll do it."

"Okay," Trent said. "We'll need some things." He took a deep breath and began explaining what they were.

Once they were convened around the crack at the end of the third-floor hallway, Trent held Lissa up so she could shine the beam of a small flashlight into the crack. They could all see the metal.

He turned to Laurie and asked her to give him the drill.

Brian and Lissa exchanged an uneasy glance as Laurie passed it over. They were afraid Daddy Lew would notice if they drilled the holes in the wall outside his study.

"Look," Trent said, holding the drill out so they could get a good look. "This is what they call a needle-point drillbit. See how tiny it is? And since we're only going to drill behind the pictures, I don't think we have to worry."

There were about a dozen framed prints along the third-floor hallway, half of them beyond the study door, on the way to the closet at the end where the suitcases were stored.

"He doesn't even look *at* them, let alone *behind* them," Laurie agreed.

She took down the picture that hung closest to the small crack in the plaster and gave it to Brian. Trent drilled.

The drillbit went easily into the wall, and the hole it made was every bit as tiny as promised.

After a dozen or so turns of the drill's handle, Trent stopped and reversed, pulling the bit free.

"Why'd you quit?" Brian asked.

"Hit something hard."

"More metal?" Lissa asked.

"I think so. Sure wasn't wood. Let's see." He shone the light in and cocked his head this way and that before shaking it decisively. "My head's too big. Let's boost Lissa."

Laurie and Trent lifted her up and Brian handed her the flashlight. Lissa squinted for a time, then said, "Just like in the crack I found."

"Okay," Trent said. "Next picture."

The drill hit metal behind the second, and the third, as well. Behind the fourth—by this time they were quite close to the door of Lew's study—it went all the way in before Trent pulled it out. This time when she was boosted up, Lissa told them she saw "pink stuff."

"Yeah, the insulation I told you about," Trent said to Laurie. "Let's try the other side of the hall."

They had to drill behind four pictures on the east side of the corridor before they struck first wood-lath and then insulation behind the plaster... and as they were rehanging the last picture, they heard the out-of-tune snarl of Lew's elderly Porsche turning in to the driveway.

Trent quickly hung the picture.

"Go!" he whispered. "Downstairs! TV room!"

The back door slammed downstairs as Lew came in.

There was a moment of almost unbearable suspense when the only sounds were the kids' footsteps on the stairs, and then Lew bawled up at them from the kitchen: "KEEP IT DOWN, CAN'T YOU? YOUR MOTHER'S TAKING A NAP!"

And if that doesn't wake her up, Laurie thought, *nothing will.*

During the next week and a half, they drilled other small holes around the house when there was no one around to see them: holes behind posters in their various rooms, behind the refrigerator in the pantry, in the downstairs closets. Trent even drilled one in the dining room wall, high up in one corner where the shadows never quite left. He stood on top of the stepladder while Laurie held it steady.

There was no more metal anywhere. Just lath.

The children forgot about it for a little while.

One day about a month later, after Lew had gone back to teaching full-time, Brian came to Trent and told him there was another crack in the plaster on the third floor, and that he could see more metal behind it. Trent and Lissa came at once. Laurie was still in school, at band practice.

As on the occasion of the first crack, their mother was lying down with a headache. Lew's temper had improved once he was back at school, but he'd had a crackerjack argument with their mother the night before, about a party he wanted to have for fellow faculty members in the History Department. If there was anything the former Mrs. Bradbury hated and feared, it was playing hostess at faculty parties. Lew had insisted on this one, however, and she had finally given in. Now she was lying in the shadowy bedroom with a damp towel over her eyes while Lew was presumably passing around invitations in the faculty lounge.

The new crack was on the west side of the hallway, between the study door and the stairwell.

"You sure you saw metal in there?" Trent asked. "We *checked* this side, Bri."

"Look for yourself," Brian said, and Trent did. There was no need for a flashlight; this crack was wider, and there was no question about the metal at the bottom of it.

After a long look, Trent told them he had to go to the hardware store right away.

"Why?" Lissa asked.

"I want to get some plaster. I don't want him to see that crack." He hesitated, then added: "And I especially don't want him to see the metal inside it."

Lissa frowned at him. "Why not, Trent?"

But Trent didn't exactly know. At least, not yet.

They started drilling again, and this time they found metal behind *all* the walls on the third floor, including Lew's study. Trent snuck in there one afternoon with the drill while Lew was at the college and their mother was out shopping for the upcoming faculty party.

Their mother looked very pale and drawn these days—even Lissa had noticed—but when any of the children asked her if she was okay, she would always flash a troubling, overbright smile and tell them never better.

One of Lew's advanced degrees was hanging on the wall over his desk in a frame. While the other children clustered outside the door, nearly vomiting with terror, Trent removed the framed degree from its hook, laid it on the desk, and drilled a pinhole in the center of the square where it had been. Two inches in, the drill hit metal.

Trent carefully rehung the degree—making very sure it wasn't crooked—and came back out.

They drilled holes at intervals along the stairs to the second floor and found metal behind these walls, too. The metal continued roughly halfway down the second-floor hallway as it proceeded toward the front of the house. It was behind the walls of Brian's room, but behind only one wall of Laurie's.

"It hasn't finished growing in here," Laurie said darkly.

Trent looked at her, surprised. "Huh?"

Before she could reply, Brian had a brainstorm.

"Try the floor, Trent!" he said. "See if it's there, too."

Trent shrugged, then drilled into the floor of Laurie's room. The drill went in all the way with no resistance, but when he peeled back the rug at the foot of his own bed and tried it there, he soon encountered solid steel…or solid whatever-it-was.

Then, at Lissa's insistence, he stood on a stool and drilled up into the ceiling.

"Boink," he said after a few moments. "More metal. Let's quit for the day."

Laurie was the only one who saw how deeply troubled Trent looked.

That night after lights-out, it was Trent who came to Laurie's room, and Laurie didn't even pretend to be sleepy. The truth was, neither of them had been sleeping very well for the last couple of weeks.

"What did you mean?" Trent whispered, sitting down beside her.

"About what?" Laurie asked, getting up on one elbow.

"You said it hadn't finished growing in your room. What did you mean?"

"Come on, Trent—you're not dumb."

"No, I'm not," he agreed. "Maybe I just want to hear you say it, Sprat."

"If you call me that, you never will."

"Okay. Laurie, Laurie, Laurie. You satisfied?"

"Yes. That stuff's growing all over the house." She paused. "No, that's not right. It's growing *under* the house."

"That's not right, either."

Laurie thought about it, then sighed. "Okay," she said. "It's growing *in* the house. It's *stealing* the house. Is that good enough, Mr. Smarty?"

"Stealing the house..." Trent sat quietly beside her on the bed. At last he nodded and flashed the smile she loved. "Yes—that's good enough."

"Whatever you call it, it acts like it's alive."

Trent nodded.

"But that isn't the worst."

"What is?"

"It's *sneaking*." Her eyes were big and frightened. "That's the part I really don't like. I don't know what started it or what it means, and I really don't care. But it's *sneaking*.

"I feel like something's going to happen, Trent, only I don't know what, and it's like being in a nightmare you can't get all the way out of. Does it feel like that to you sometimes?"

"A little, yeah. But I *know* something's going to happen. I might even know what."

She bolted to a sitting position and grabbed his hands. "You *know?* What? What is it?"

"I can't be sure," Trent said, getting up. "I *think* I know, but I'm not ready to say what I think yet. I have to do some more looking."

"If we drill many more holes, the house is going to fall down!"

"I didn't say *drilling*, I said *looking*."

"Looking for *what?*"

"For something that isn't here yet—that hasn't grown yet. But when it does, I don't think it will be able to hide."

"*Tell* me, Trent!"

"Not yet," he said, and planted a small, quick kiss on her cheek. "Besides—curiosity killed the Sprat."

"I *hate* you!" she cried in a low voice, and flopped back down with the sheet over her head. But she felt better for having talked with Trent, and slept better than she had for a week.

Trent found what he was looking for two days before the big party. As the oldest, he perhaps should have noticed that his mother had begun to look alarmingly unhealthy, rubbing at her temples all the time, although she denied—almost in a panic—that she had a migraine.

He did not notice these things, however. He was too busy looking.

He went through every closet in the big old house at least three times; through the crawlspace above Lew's study five or six times; through the big old cellar half a dozen times.

It was in the cellar that he finally found it.

This was not to say he hadn't found peculiar things in other places; he most certainly had. There was a knob of stainless steel poking out of the ceiling of a second-floor closet. A curved metal armature of some kind had burst through the side of the luggage closet on the third floor. It was a dim, polished gray…until he touched it. When he did that, it flushed a dusky rose color, and he heard a faint but powerful humming sound deep in the wall. He snatched his hand back as if the armature were hot and the curved metal thing went gray again. The humming stopped at once.

The day before, in the attic, he had observed a cobweb of thin, interlaced cables growing in a low dark corner under the eave. Trent had been crawling around on his hands and knees when he had suddenly spied this amazing phenomenon. He froze in place, staring through a tangle of hair as the cables spun themselves out of nothing at all (or so it looked, anyway), met, wrapped around each other so tightly that they seemed to merge, and then continued spreading until they reached the floor, where they drilled in and anchored themselves in dreamy little puffs of sawdust. They seemed to be creating some sort of limber bracework, and it looked as if it would be *very* strong, able to hold the house together through a lot of buffeting and hard knocks.

What buffeting, though?

What hard knocks?

Again, Trent thought he knew. It was hard to believe, but he thought he knew.

Far beyond the workshop area and the furnace, there was a little closet at the north end of the cellar, which their real father had called his "wine cellar."

Lew came in here even less frequently than he went into the workshop; he didn't drink wine and their mother no longer drank wine either.

There was a padlock on the wine cellar door, but the key hung right next to it.

He was not much surprised by the sour whiff of spilled wine that greeted him as he approached the door; it was just more proof of what he and Laurie already knew—the changes were winding themselves quietly all through the house. He opened the door, and although what he saw frightened him, it didn't really surprise him.

Metal constructions had burst through two of the wine cellar's walls, tearing apart the racks with their diamond-shaped compartments and pushing the bottles onto the floor, where they had broken.

Like the cables in the attic crawlspace, whatever was forming here—growing, to use Laurie's word—hadn't finished yet. It spun itself into being in sheens of light that hurt Trent's eyes and made him feel a little sick to his stomach.

No cables here, however, and no curved struts. What was growing in his real father's forgotten wine cellar looked like cabinets and consoles and instrument panels. And as he looked, vague shapes humped themselves up in the metal like the heads of excited snakes, gained focus, became dials and levers and readouts. There were also a few blinking lights. Some of these actually began to blink as he looked at them.

A low sighing sound accompanied this act of creation.

Trent took one cautious step farther into the little room; an especially bright red light, or series of them, had caught his eye.

The lights were numbers. They were under a glass strip on a metal construct that was spinning its way out of a console. This new thing looked like some sort of chair, although no one sitting in it would have been very comfortable. At least, no one with a *human* shape, Trent thought with a little shiver.

The glass strip was in one of the arms of this twisted chair—if it *was* a chair. And the numbers had perhaps caught his eye because they were changing.

72:34:18

became

72:34:17

and then

72:34:16.

Trent looked at his watch, which had a sweep second hand, and used it to confirm what his eyes had already told him. The chair might or might not be really a chair, but the numbers under the glass strip were a digital clock. It was running backwards. Counting down, to be perfectly accurate. And what would happen when that readout finally went from

00:00:01

to

00:00:00

some three days from this very afternoon?

He was pretty sure he knew. Every kid knows one or two things happen when a backwards-running clock finally reads zeros across the board: an explosion or a lift-off.

Trent thought there was too much equipment, too many gadgets, for it to be an explosion.

He thought something had gotten into the house while they were in England. Some sort of spore, perhaps, that had drifted through space for a billion years before being caught in the gravitational pull of the earth, spiraling down through the atmosphere like a bit of milkweed fluff caught in a mild breeze, and finally falling into the chimney of a house in Titusville, Indiana.

Into the *Bradburys'* house in Titusville, Indiana.

It might have been something else entirely, of course, but the spore idea *felt* right to Trent, and although he was the oldest of the Bradbury kids, he was still young enough to believe completely in his own perceptions and intuitions. And in the end, it didn't really matter, did it? What *mattered* was what had *happened.*

And, of course, what was *going* to happen.

When Trent left the wine cellar this time, he not only snapped the padlock's arm closed, but took the key as well.

Something terrible happened at Lew's faculty party. It happened at quarter of nine, only forty-five minutes or so after the first guests arrived.

"What's the matter with you?" Trent and Laurie heard him yelling at her, and when Trent felt Laurie's hand creep into his like a small, cold mouse, he held it tightly. "Don't you know what people are going to say about this? Don't you know how people in the department *talk?* I mean, *really,* Catherine."

Their mother's only reply was soft, helpless sobbing, and for just one moment Trent felt a horrible, unwilling burst of hate for her. Why had she married him in the first place? Didn't she deserve this for being such a fool?

Ashamed of himself, he pushed the thought away, made it gone, and turned to Laurie.

"Great party, huh?" she whispered, tears pouring down her cheeks.

"Right, Sprat," he said, and hugged her so she could cry against his shoulder without being heard. "It'll make my top-ten list at the end of the year, no sweat."

It seemed that their mother had been lying to everyone. She had been in the grip of a screaming-blue migraine for not just a day or two days but this time for the last two weeks. During that time she had eaten next to nothing and lost fifteen pounds. She had been serving canapés to Stephen Krutchmer, the head of the History Department, and his wife when the colors went out of everything and the world suddenly swam away from her. She had rolled bonelessly forward, spilling a whole tray of Chinese pork rolls onto the front of Mrs. Krutchmer's expensive dress.

Brian and Lissa had heard the commotion and had come creeping down the stairs in their pajamas to see what was going on, although all four children had been strictly forbidden by Daddy Lew to leave the upper floors of the house once the party began.

When they saw their mother on the floor in a circle of kneeling, concerned faculty members, they had forgotten their stepfather's firm order and had run in, Lissa crying, Brian bellowing in excited dismay.

"Mom! Mommy!" Brian cried, shaking her. "*Mommy!* Wake up!"

Mrs. Evans stirred and moaned.

"Get upstairs," Lew said coldly. "Both of you."

When they showed no signs of obeying, Lew put his hand on Lissa's shoulder and tightened it until she squeaked with pain.

"I'll take care of this," he said through teeth so tightly clamped they refused to entirely unlock even to speak. "You and your brother go upstairs right n—"

"Take your hand off her," Trent said clearly.

Lew turned toward the archway between the living room and the hallway. Trent and Laurie stood there, side by side. Trent was as pale as his stepfather, but his face was calm and set.

"I want you to go upstairs," Lew said. "All four of you. There's nothing here to concern you. Nothing to concern you at all."

"Get your hand off Lissa," Trent said.

"And get away from our mother," Laurie said.

Now Mrs. Evans was sitting up, her hands to her head, looking around dazedly. The headache had popped like a balloon, leaving her disoriented and weak but finally out of the agony she had endured for the last fourteen days. She knew she had done something terrible, embarrassed Lew, perhaps even *disgraced* him, but for the moment she was too grateful that the pain had stopped to care. The shame would come later. Now she only wanted to go upstairs—very slowly—and lie down.

"You'll be punished for this," Lew said, looking at his four stepchildren in the nearly perfect shocked silence of the living room. "I'm sorry for their misbehavior," he said to the room at large. "My wife is a bit lax with them, I'm afraid. What they need is a good English nanny—"

"Don't be an idiot, Lew," Mrs. Krutchmer said. "Your wife fainted. They were concerned, that's all. Children *should* care about their mother. And a husband about his wife."

Trent and Laurie assisted their mother up the stairs, and Lissa and Brian trailed along behind.

The party went on. The incident was more or less papered over, as unpleasant incidents at parties usually are. Mrs. Evans was asleep almost as soon as her head touched the pillow, and the children heard Lew downstairs, enjoying the party without her.

He never once broke away to come up and check on her.

After the last guest had been shown out, he walked heavily upstairs and poked his head into Trent's room and measured the children with his gaze.

"I knew you'd all be in here," he said with a satisfied little nod. "Conspiring. You're going to be punished, you know. Yes indeed. Tomorrow. Tonight I want you to go right to bed and think about it. Now go to your rooms. And no creeping around, either."

Neither Lissa nor Brian did any "creeping around," certainly; they were too exhausted to do anything but fall asleep immediately. But Laurie came back down to Trent's room in spite of Lew, and the two of them listened in silent dismay as their stepfather upbraided their mother for daring to faint at *his* party . . . and as their mother wept and offered not a word of argument or even demurral.

"Oh, Trent, what are we going to do?" Laurie asked.

Trent's face was extraordinarily pale and still. "Do?" he said. "Why, we're not going to do anything, Sprat."

"We *have* to! Trent, we *have* to! We have to help her!"

"No, we don't," Trent said. "This house is going to do it for us." He looked at his watch and calculated. "At around three thirty-four tomorrow afternoon, the house is going to do it all."

There were no punishments in the morning; Lew Evans told them he would see them in his study that night, one by one, and "mete a fair few strokes to each," and left for work.

The two younger kids were standing by the kitchen. Lissa was crying. Brian was keeping a stiff upper lip, but he was pale and there were purple pouches under his eyes. "He'll spank us," Brian said to Trent. "And he spanks *hard,* too."

"Nope," Trent said.

"But, Trent—" Lissa began.

"Listen to me," Trent said. "And listen carefully, and don't you miss a single word. It's important, and none of us can screw up."

They stared at him silently with their big green-blue eyes.

"As soon as school is out, I want you two to come right home . . . but only as far as the corner. The corner of Maple and Walnut. Have you got that?"

"Ye-ess," Lissa said hesitantly. "But why, Trent?"

"Never mind," Trent said. His eyes were sparkling dangerously. "Just be there. Stand by the mailbox. You have to be there by three o'clock, three fifteen at the *latest.* Do you understand?"

"Yes," Brian said, speaking for both of them. "We got it."

"Laurie and I will already be there, or we'll be there right after you get there."

"How are we going to do that, Trent?" Laurie asked. "We don't even get out of school until three o'clock, and I have band practice, and the bus takes—"

"We're not *going* to school today," Trent said.

"No?" Laurie was nonplussed.

Lissa was horrified. "Trent!" she said. "You can't do that! That's... that's... *hookey!*"

"And about time, too," Trent said grimly. "Now you two get ready for school. Just remember, the corner of Maple and Walnut at three o'clock, three fifteen at the absolute latest. And whatever you do, *don't come all the way home.*" He stared at Brian and Lissa fiercely. Even Laurie was frightened. "Wait for us, but don't you *dare* come back into this house," he said. "Not for *anything.*"

When the little kids were gone, Laurie seized his shirt and demanded to know what was going on.

"It has something to do with what's growing in the house, I *know* it does, and if you want me to play hookey and help you, you better tell me what it is!"

"Chill out, I'll tell you," Trent said. "And be quiet. I don't want you to wake up Mom. She'll make us go to school, and that's no good."

"Well, what *is* it? Tell me!"

"Come downstairs," Trent said. "I want to show you something."

He led her downstairs to the wine cellar.

Trent wasn't completely sure Laurie would ride along with what he had in mind—it seemed awfully... well, final... even to him—but she did. If it had just been a matter of enduring a spanking from "Daddy Lew," he didn't think she would have, but Laurie had been as deeply affected by the sight of her mother lying senseless on the living room floor as Trent had been by his stepfather's unfeeling reaction to it.

"Yeah," Laurie said bleakly. "I think we have to." She was looking at the blinking numbers on the arm of the chair. They now read

07:49:21.

The wine cellar was no longer a wine cellar at all. It stank of wine, true enough, and there were piles of shattered green glass on the floor, but it now looked like a madman's version of the control bridge on the Starship *Enterprise*. Dials whirled. Digital readouts flickered, changed, flickered again. Lights blinked and flashed.

"If we don't do something, he'll kill her," Laurie said in a low voice.

She was looking at the red numbers of the countdown.

"Not on purpose," she said. "He might even be sad. For a while, anyway. Because I think he *does* love her, sort of, and she loves him. You know—sort of. But he'll make her worse and worse. She'll get sick all the time, and then . . . one day . . ."

She broke off and looked at him, and something in her face scared Trent worse than anything in their strange, changing, *sneaking* house had been able to do.

"Tell me, Trent," she said. Her hand grasped his arm. It was very cold. "Tell me how we're going to do it."

They went up to Lew's study together and found the key in the top drawer, tucked neatly into an envelope with the word STUDY printed on it. They left the house together just as the shower on the second floor went on, meaning their mom was up.

They spent the day in the park. Although neither of them spoke of it, it was the longest day either of them had ever lived through. Twice they saw the beat cop and hid in the public toilets until he was gone. This was no time to be caught playing truant and bundled off to school.

At two thirty, they walked to the phone booth on the east side of the park.

"Do I have to?" Laurie asked. "I hate to scare her, especially after last night."

"Do you want her in the house when whatever happens, happens?" Trent asked. Laurie dropped a quarter into the telephone with no further protest.

It rang so many times that she became sure their mother had gone out. That might be good, but it might also be bad. It was certainly worrisome. If she was out it was entirely possible that she might come back before—

"Trent I don't think she's h—"

"Hello?" Mrs. Evans said in a sleepy voice.

"Oh, hi, Mom," Laurie said. "I didn't think you were there."

"I went back to bed," she said with an embarrassed little laugh. "I can't seem to get enough sleep, all of a sudden. I suppose if I'm asleep I can't think about how horrible I was last night—"

"Oh, Mom, you weren't horrible. When a person faints, it isn't because she *wants* to—"

"Laurie, why are you calling? Is everything okay?"

"Sure, Mom... well..."

Trent poked her in the ribs. Hard.

Laurie, who had been slumping, straightened up in a hurry. "I hurt myself in gym. Just... you know, a little. It's not bad."

"What did you do? You're not calling from the hospital, are you?"

"Gosh, no," Laurie said hastily. "It's just a sprained knee. Mrs. Kitt asked if you could come and bring me home early. I don't know if I can walk on it. It really hurts."

"I'll come right away. Try not to move it at all, honey."

"Don't worry, Mom, I'll be careful."

"Will you be in the nurse's office? I'll be right there."

"Thanks, Mom. Bye."

She hung up and looked at Trent. She drew in a deep breath and then let it out in a long, trembly sigh.

"That was fun," she said in a voice close to tears.

He hugged her tight. "You did great," he said.

"I wonder if she'll ever believe *me* again?" Laurie asked bitterly.

"She will," Trent said. "Come on."

They went over to the west side of the park, where they could watch Walnut Street. The day had turned cold and dim. Thunderheads were forming overhead, and a chilly wind was blowing. They waited for five endless minutes and then their mother's car passed them, heading rapidly toward Greendowne Middle School.

Laurie had Trent's hand and was pulling him back to the telephone booth again. "*You* get to call Lew."

He put in another quarter and punched the number of the History Department office. He glanced at his watch. Quarter to three. Less than an hour to go. Thunder rumbled faintly in the west.

"History Department," a woman's voice said.

"Hi. This is Trent Bradbury. I need to speak with my stepfather, Lewis Evans, please."

"Professor Evans is in class," the secretary said, "but he'll be out at—"

"I know, he's got Modern British History until three thirty. But you better get him, just the same. It's an emergency. It concerns his wife." Then he added: "My mom."

There was a long pause, and Trent felt a moment of faint alarm. It was as if she were thinking of refusing or dismissing him, emergency or no emergency, and that was most definitely not in the plan.

"He's in Oglethorpe, right next door," she said finally. "I'll get him myself. I'll have him call as soon as—"

"No, I have to hold on," Trent said.

"But—"

"Please, will you just stop messing with me and go get him?" he asked, allowing a ragged, harried note into his voice. It wasn't hard.

"All right," the secretary said. "If you could tell me the nature of the—"

"No," Trent said.

"Well?" Laurie asked.

"I'm on hold. They're getting him."

"What if he doesn't come?"

Trent shrugged. "Then we're sunk. But he'll come. You wait and see."

"We left it until awful late."

Trent nodded. They had left it until awful late.

"Why doesn't he answer the darn *phone?*" Laurie asked, looking at her watch.

"He will," Trent said, and then their stepfather did.

"Hello?"

"It's Trent, Lew. Mom's in your study. Her headache must have come back, because she fainted. I can't wake her up. You better come home right away."

Trent was not surprised at his stepfather's first stated object of concern.

"My study? My *study?* What the hell was she doing in there?"

In spite of his anger, Trent's voice came out calmly. "Cleaning, I think." And then tossed the ultimate bait to a man who cared a great deal more for work than his wife: "There are papers all over the floor."

"I'll be right there," Lew rapped, and then added: "If there are any windows open in there, shut them, for God's sake. There's a storm coming." He hung up without saying goodbye.

"Well?" Laurie asked.

"He's on his way," Trent said, and laughed grimly.

They ran back to the intersection of Maple and Walnut. The sky had grown very dark now, and the sound of thunder had become almost constant. As they reached the mailbox on the corner, the streetlights along Maple Street began to come on.

Lissa and Brian hadn't arrived yet.

"I want to come with you, Trent," Laurie said, her eyes swimming with unshed tears.

"No way," Trent said. "Wait here for Brian and Lissa."

At their names, Laurie turned and looked down Walnut Street and saw them coming, hurrying along with lunchboxes bouncing in their hands.

"Good. The three of you go behind Mrs. Redland's hedge there and wait for Lew to pass. Then you can come up the street, *but don't go in the house and don't let them, either.* Wait for me outside."

"I'm afraid, Trent." The tears had begun to spill down her cheeks now.

"Me too, Sprat," he said, and kissed her swiftly on the forehead. "But it'll all be over soon."

Before she could say anything else, Trent went running up the street toward the Bradburys' house on Maple Street. He glanced at his watch as he ran. It was twelve past three.

The house had a still, hot air that scared him. It was as if gunpowder had been spilled in every corner and people he could not see were standing by to light unseen fuses. He imagined the clock in the wine cellar ticking relentlessly away, now reading

00:19:06.

What if Lew *was* late?

Trent raced up to the third floor through the still, combustible air. He imagined he could feel the house stirring now, coming alive as the countdown neared its conclusion.

He went into Lew's study, opened two or three file cabinets and desk drawers at random, and threw the papers he found all over the floor. He was just finishing when he heard the Porsche coming up the street.

Trent stepped out of the office and rammed his hand into his pocket for the key, but it was empty except for an old, crumpled lunch ticket.

I must have lost it running up the street. It must have bounced right out of my pocket.

He stood there, sweating and frozen, as the Porsche squealed into the driveway. Its engine cut out. The driver's door opened and slammed shut. Lew's footsteps ran for the back door. Thunder crumped like an artillery shell in the sky, a stroke of bright lightning forked through the gloom, and, somewhere deep in the house, a powerful motor turned over, uttered a low, muffled bark, and began to hum.

What do I do? What CAN *I do? He's bigger than me! If I try to hit him over the head, he'll—*

He slipped his left hand into his other pocket, and his thoughts broke off as it touched the old-fashioned metal teeth of the key. At some point during the long afternoon in the park, he must have transferred it from one pocket to the other without even being aware of it.

Gasping, heart galloping in his stomach and throat as well as in his chest, Trent faded back down the hall to the luggage closet, stepped inside, and pulled the accordion-style doors most of the way shut in front of him.

Lew was galumphing up the stairs, bawling his wife's name over and over at the top of his voice. Trent saw him appear, hair standing up in spikes, his tie askew, big drops of sweat standing out on his broad, intelligent forehead, eyes squinted down to furious little slits.

"*Catherine!*" he bawled, and he ran down the hall into the office.

Trent was out of the luggage closet and running soundlessly back down the hall. He would have just one chance. If he missed the keyhole ... if the key failed to turn ...

If either of those things happens, I'll fight with him, he had time to think. *If I can't send him alone, I'll make damn sure to take him with me.*

He grabbed the door and banged it shut. He caught one glimpse of Lew's startled face. Then the key was in the lock. He twisted it, and the bolt shot across an instant before Lew struck the door.

"Hey!" Lew shouted. "Hey, what are you doing? Where's Catherine? Let me out of here!"

The knob twisted back and forth. Then it stopped and Lew rained a fusillade of blows on the door.

"Let me out of here right now, Trent Bradbury, before you get the worst beating of your life!"

Trent backed slowly across the hall. When his shoulders struck the far wall, he gasped. The key dropped from his fingers. Now that it was done, reaction set in. The world began to look wavery, as if he were under water, and he had to fight to keep from fainting himself. Only now, with Lew locked in, his mother sent off on a wild-goose chase, and the other kids safely tucked away behind Mrs. Redland's overgrown yew hedge, did he realize that he had never really expected it would work at all. If "Daddy Lew" was surprised to find himself locked in, Trent Bradbury was absolutely amazed.

The doorknob of the study twisted back and forth in short sharp half-circles.

"LET ME OUT NOW!"

"I'll let you out at quarter of four, Lew," Trent said in an uneven, trembling voice, and then a little giggle escaped him. "If you're still *here* at quarter of four, that is."

Then, from downstairs: "Trent? Trent, are you all right?"

Dear God, that was Laurie.

"Are you, Trent?"

And Lissa!

"Hey, *Trent!* Y'okay?"

And Brian.

Trent looked at his watch and was horrified to see it was 3:31 ... going on 3:32. *And suppose his watch was slow?*

"*Get out!*" he screamed down to them. "*Get out of this house!*"

The third-floor hallway seemed to stretch out before him like taffy; the faster he ran, the farther it seemed to stretch ahead of him. Lew rained blows on the door and curses on the air; thunder boomed; and from deep within the house came the ever-more-urgent sound of machines waking to life.

He reached the stairwell at last and hurried down, hurtling down the stairs to the first floor, where his brother and two sisters waited, looking up at him.

"*Out!*" he screamed, grabbing them, shoving them toward the open door and the stormy blackness outside. "*Quick!*"

"Trent, what's happening?" Brian asked. "What's happening to the *house?* It's *shaking!*"

It was, too—a deep vibration that rose up through the floor and rattled Trent's eyeballs in their sockets. Plaster dust began to sift down into his hair.

"No time! Out! Fast! Laurie, help me!"

Trent swept Brian into his arms. Laurie grabbed Lissa and stumbled out the door.

Thunder bammed. Lightning twisted across the sky. The wind that had been gasping earlier now began to roar like a dragon.

Trent heard an earthquake building under the house. As he ran out through the door with Brian, he saw electric-blue light shoot out through the narrow cellar windows. It cut across the lawn in rays that looked almost solid. He heard the glass break. And, just as he passed through the door, he felt the house *rising* under his feet.

He jumped down the front steps and grabbed Laurie's arm. They stumble-staggered down the walk to the street, which was now as black as night with the coming of the storm.

There they turned back and watched it happen.

The house on Maple Street seemed to gather itself. It no longer looked straight and solid. Huge cracks ran out from it, not only in the cement walk but in the earth surrounding it. The lawn pulled apart. Roots strained blackly upward below the green. The whole front yard seemed to become bubble-shaped, as if it were straining to hold the house before which it had spread for so long.

Trent cast his eyes up to the third floor, where the light in Lew's study still shone. Trent thought the sound of breaking glass had come—was coming—from up there. It was a year later that Laurie told him she was quite sure she had heard their stepfather screaming.

The foundation of the house first crumbled, then cracked, then sundered with a croak of exploding mortar. Brilliant cold blue fire lanced out. The children covered their eyes and staggered back. Engines screamed. The earth pulled up and up in a last agonized holding action...and then let go. Suddenly the house was a foot above the ground, resting on a pad of bright blue fire.

It was a perfect lift-off.

The house rose slowly at first, then began to gather speed. It thundered upward on its flaring pad of blue fire, the front door clapping madly back and forth as it went.

The house reached a height of thirty yards, seemed to poise itself for its great leap upward, then *blasted* into the rushing spate of night-black clouds.

It was gone.

"Look out, Trent!" Laurie cried out a second or two later, and shoved him hard enough to knock him over. The rubber-backed welcome mat thwacked into the street where he had been standing.

Trent looked at Laurie. Laurie looked back.

"That would've killed you if it'd hit you on the head," she told him, "so you just better not call me Sprat anymore, Trent."

He looked at her solemnly for several seconds, then began to giggle. Laurie joined in. So did the little ones. Brian took one of Trent's hands; Lissa took the other. They helped pull him to his feet, and then the four of them stood together, looking at the smoking cellar hole in the middle of the shattered lawn. People were coming out of their houses now.

"Wow," Brian said reverently. "Our house took off, Trent."

"Yeah," Trent said.

Trent and Laurie put their arms around each other and began to shriek with mingled laughter and horror...and that was when the rain began to pelt down.

The Bradbury children sat down on the curb, Trent and Laurie in the middle, Brian and Lissa on the sides.

Laurie leaned toward Trent and whispered in his ear: "We're free."

"It's better than that," Trent said. "*She* is."

Then he put his arms around all of them—by stretching, he could just manage—and they sat on the curb in the pouring rain and waited for their mother to come home.

Original Introduction to *The Mysteries of Harris Burdick*

I first saw the drawings in this book a year ago, in the home of a man named Peter Wenders. Though Mr. Wenders is retired now, he once worked for a children's book publisher, choosing the stories and pictures that would be turned into books.

Thirty years ago a man called at Peter Wenders's office, introducing himself as Harris Burdick. Mr. Burdick explained that he had written fourteen stories and had drawn many pictures for each one. He'd brought with him just one drawing from each story, to see if Wenders liked his work.

Peter Wenders was fascinated by the drawings. He told Burdick he would like to read the stories that went with them as soon as possible. The artist agreed to bring the stories the next morning. He left the fourteen drawings with Wenders. But he did not return the next day. Or the day after that. Harris Burdick was never heard from again. Over the years, Wenders tried to find out who Burdick was and what had happened to him, but he discovered nothing. To this day Harris Burdick remains a complete mystery.

His disappearance is not the only mystery left behind. What were the stories that went with these drawings? There are some clues. Burdick had written a title and caption for each picture. When I told Peter Wenders how difficult it was to look at the drawings and their captions without imagining a story, he smiled and left the room. He returned with a dust-covered cardboard box. Inside were dozens of stories, all inspired by the Burdick drawings. They'd been written years ago by Wenders's children and their friends.

I spent the rest of my visit reading these stories. They were remarkable, some bizarre, some funny, some downright scary. In the hope that other children will be inspired by them, the Burdick drawings are reproduced here for the first time.

Chris Van Allsburg
Providence, Rhode Island, 1984

HB

About the Authors

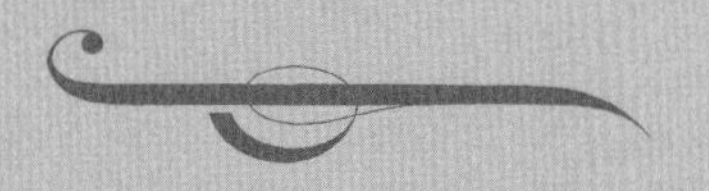

SHERMAN ALEXIE is the author of several novels and collections of short fiction, including the National Book Award winner *The Absolutely True Diary of a Part-Time Indian* (2007) and *War Dances,* winner of the 2010 PEN/Faulkner Award for Fiction. Mr. Alexie lives in Seattle, Washington.

M. T. ANDERSON is the author of many books for young people, including *Feed,* which was a finalist for the National Book Award and was a Boston Globe–Horn Book Honor book, *The Astonishing Life of Octavian Nothing, Traitor to the Nation, Volume I: The Pox Party,* which received the Printz Honor and the National Book Award, and *The Astonishing Life of Octavian Nothing, Traitor to the Nation, Volume II: The Kingdom on the Waves,* which was also a Printz Honor recipient. Mr. Anderson lives in Boston, Massachusetts.

KATE DiCAMILLO is the author of *The Tale of Despereaux,* which was awarded the Newbery Medal, *Because of Winn-Dixie,* a Newbery Honor book, *The Magician's Elephant, The Miraculous Journey of Edward Tulane,* and six books starring Mercy Watson, including the Theodor Seuss Geisel Honor book *Mercy Watson Goes for a Ride.* She coauthored the Theodor Seuss Geisel Award–winning *Bink and Gollie* with Alison McGhee. She lives in Minneapolis, Minnesota.

CORY DOCTOROW is a science-fiction author, activist, journalist, and blogger—as well as the co-editor of Boing Boing (boingboing.net) and the author of several books, including the best-selling novel *Little Brother.* He lives in London, England.

JULES FEIFFER has won a Pulitzer Prize for his cartoons, an Obie for his plays, and an Academy Award for animation. He has written and illustrated many books for children, including *The Man in the Ceiling* and *Bark, George,* as well as illustrated the classic *The Phantom Tollbooth.*

STEPHEN KING is one of the world's most successful writers. His works include *Carrie, The Shining, The Stand,* and *It.* He has won many awards and honors, including several Bram Stoker Awards.

TABITHA KING is the author of several novels. A social activist, she's involved with many boards and philanthropic foundations. She lives in Maine and Florida with her husband, Stephen King.

LOIS LOWRY is the author of many beloved books for children. She received Newbery Medals for two of her novels, *Number the Stars* and *The Giver.* She has received countless other honors, among them the Boston Globe–Horn Book Award and the Regina Medal. She lives in Cambridge, Massachusetts.

GREGORY MAGUIRE is the author of many books for adults, including the bestseller *Wicked,* and more than a dozen novels for children. Mr. Maguire has been the recipient of several awards and fellowships. He lives in Concord, Massachusetts.

WALTER DEAN MYERS is the critically acclaimed author of more than eighty books for children and young adults. His award-winning body of work includes *Sunrise over Fallujah, Fallen Angels,* and *Monster.* Mr. Myers has received two Newbery Honors, the Printz Award, and five Coretta Scott King Awards, and has been a three-time finalist for the National Book Award. Mr. Myers lives in Jersey City, New Jersey.

LINDA SUE PARK is the author of the Newbery Medal winner *A Single Shard,* as well as numerous other novels, picture books, and poetry. She lives in Rochester, New York.

LOUIS SACHAR is the author of *Holes,* which was the winner of the Newbery Award, the Boston Globe–Horn Book Award, and the National Book Award. He is also the author of the popular Marvin Redpost series, the Wayside School series, and most recently *The Cardturner.* Mr. Sachar lives in Austin, Texas.

JON SCIESZKA was appointed the first National Ambassador for Young People's Literature in 2008. He is the author of several best-selling children's titles, including *The Stinky Cheese Man,* which received a Caldecott Honor, *The True Story of the Three Little Pigs,* and the Time Warp Trio series. Mr. Scieszka is the founder of Guys Read, a nonprofit literacy organization.

LEMONY SNICKET is the author of several other unpleasant stories, including those in the best-selling A Series of Unfortunate Events books and *The Lump of Coal.*

CHRIS VAN ALLSBURG is the winner of two Caldecott Medals, for *Jumanji* and *The Polar Express,* as well as the recipient of a Caldecott Honor for *The Garden of Abdul Gasazi.* The author and illustrator of numerous picture books for children, he has also received the National Book Award and the Regina Medal for lifetime achievement in children's literature.

BOCA RATON PUBLIC LIBRARY
3 3656 3000995 3